Free to Drink the Wind

A Misty West Mystery

By

Ruth Foreman

December, 2003

To Halle
Best wishes —
Ruth Foreman

Beaver Books

ISBN: 1-4107-6855-4 (e-book)
ISBN: 1-4107-6854-6 (Paperback)

brary of Congress Control Number: 2003094697

his book is printed on acid free paper.

ted in the United States of America
Bloomington, IN

over image © 2003 clipart.com

Dedication/Thanks

This book is dedicated to Karen and Anna—who love horses.

Many thanks to all of the following:

- my husband who loves the Sandhills of Nebraska

- Dr. Richard Jaggers for his interest and medical advice

- the Alliance Book Group for their excellent ideas and critical expertise

- Jody Mischnick and her eighth-grade class for their help and feedback

- friends and family who offered constant encouragement

- the Arabian Horse Registry of America, Inc.

- and the extraordinary people who have written about or photographed beautiful Arabian horses.

Prologue

It had been a long trip. Home never looked so good. He had lost it a few miles back—went to sleep on the sandy trail leading to the ranch—wandered off over the prairie. It was a bumpy trek for the truck and trailer before he finally got back onto the road. Probably a good thing his arms and legs hurt so much from driving, or he never could have stayed awake at all after he left the interstate.

He angled the pickup and its trailer carelessly in front of the barn, and with a great sigh, shoved the gearshift into *PARK* and turned the key to kill the engine. He sat for a few heartbeats, took a deep breath, then opened the door and jumped awkwardly from the cab. He wished he hadn't. His bad knee was stiff, and it buckled from the jolt. It took a while to get upright, but finally he stood—a stringy, aging cowboy whose jeans almost slipped past his shirttail when he stretched his arms in the air to take away the ache from the road.

A rough, low whinny came then through the night from the fifth-wheel trailer that was attached to the bed of the pickup. The man relieved his nagging bladder while leaning against the fender of the truck, then he limped his way to the back, opened the trailer door, and pulled the ramp in place. Painfully, he climbed inside, detached the stallion's halter from the front pin and backed the tired horse out of the trailer onto the gravel.

They took two miserable turns around the yard, then he tied the animal to the back of the trailer, so he could check him over in the misty yellow glow of the yard light. Wearily, he leaned his shoulder against the horse's shoulder to shift the animal's weight to the other side, then he squeezed the back of the leg he wanted to lift. The stallion raised his foot, so the man could examine it.

After he had seen to all four hooves, he was reassured that the Mexican farrier he had awakened from his siesta outside Trinidad in southern Colorado had done his job well; the shoes had been removed, and each hoof had been expertly trimmed and cleaned. Firmly he stroked the iridescent darkness of the great animal's back, then he bent to run his hand over the horse's hocks, knees and forearms. The slender legs were quivering slightly, but the horse seemed solid otherwise. He couldn't detect any swelling. If there had been more time before they left, he would have re-wrapped the stallion's elegant legs in fresh soft cotton under the elastic support bandages, but at the time, he was under pressure. He felt he just couldn't take the chance, because he was in a hurry and might do a poor job. The horse's veins were so close to the surface, and a bad wrapping could cause circulation problems.

Thankfully, the old man took up the halter rope, and as he leaned his head on the smooth pillow of the big animal's shoulder, he took a deep breath, relishing the rank, sweet smell of his coat. Tenderly, he stroked the stallion's muzzle as if to say, "I'm sorry." The man knew it wasn't right, asking a horse to stand in a trailer for almost two days with only a few short walks for relief, but there hadn't been any other way of getting him here. He and the horse had been running from something so underhanded that the back of the man's neck kinked up and he wanted to kick something whenever he thought about it.

Holding tight to the halter, he drew the animal's broad forehead down to his own for a few seconds, then led him over to the horse tank and tied him there so he could drink. When the horse raised his head from the tank, John walked him over to the corral behind the horse barn. He opened the gate, led the horse through, and closed it behind them. He and the horse then hobbled to the far end of the split-rail enclosure where he opened the gate that led to the winter pasture.

It was a good place for this horse—a mid-size ranch in what some smug city people would say was the middle of nowhere—20,000 acres of rich native grasses dotted with stubborn clumps of prickly yuccas and a smattering of sage. To those people his place would seem immense and boundless, but it was really just a decent size speck in the miles and miles of the rolling sand hills of what was once the vast ocean of Nebraska. The tired man smiled slightly as he worked his hands purposefully, slowly, up the lead rope to the halter, unbuckled it and freed the horse.

"Git," he said softly as he smacked the stallion's rump. "Lots a friends and some a your cousins waitin' out there." He pushed testily at the horse's thigh when it didn't move. "Go on now, but jist don't be too hard on the ladies." The horse stepped aside, paced a few yards, then stood motionless, sniffing the sharp night air. A cold autumn half-moon silvered the grassy dunes beyond the corral, and in the east, the first gray light of the new day was creeping over the horizon. The cowboy hooted and slapped his hat on the fence. "Git!" he repeated. Finally, warily, the tired horse retreated at a trot. When the man could no longer make him out in the great shadows that hovered against the hills, he turned to go to the house—where he threw off his boots and collapsed onto his familiar, unmade bed.

Chapter One

Misty squinted to keep the dust out of her eyes. She was headed up a narrow, no-name path worn by mule deer and coyotes—up the bluff the old-timers called Long Ridge. Pesky gusts swirled the dirt out of the crevices in the sandstone, and soon a new wind drilled its cold breath through the denim of her jacket. She shivered, then pulled a padded vest from her saddle pack and zipped it tight as her horse stepped up to the pancake of the summit.

Once settled at the top, she turned in the saddle to look below. There had been some rain in the early fall, but it had been a dry summer. The native grasses were brown and the wildflowers scarce, but the scene before her was still breathtaking in spite of what might have been. The sky was an unblemished sapphire, brilliant in the forenoon, and the hills were dappled with lop-sided ponds, lines of bright yellow cottonwoods, and clusters of cedars and junipers.

In the distance, she could see the Diamond W. Over the years ribbons of paths and roads had been worn to wind about—leading from one pasture to another—and from one structure to another. The home place seemed to have been tossed at random just off Blue Water Creek. The ranch had been in her family ever since her great-great-grandfather and grandmother had homesteaded in central Nebraska in the late 1800's. They had built the rambling house where she lived with her two brothers and her father—and sometimes her mother—a two-story prairie-style

1

stucco with a large chimney in the middle and covered decks in front and back.

Claire and Charlie Cooper's house was to the west. Newer than the main house, it had been manufactured in a town far east of the Diamond W, then pulled to the ranch by hulking truck-tractors, each hauling half a house. Misty remembered the day they had joined the two pieces and set it on the basement. The little gray house with its pitched roof had reminded her of the houses in her Monopoly set. The Coopers had lived and worked on the ranch for ten years or more now. Two bedrooms had been added, and the house had been painted the same nut color as the big house.

A split-rail fence enclosed the other buildings. Behind the Cooper's house, to the north, lay a barn-like two-story that was a bunkhouse for the extra help the ranch employed from time to time. Between were barns and metal buildings that were cloisters for livestock and shelter for all the machinery it took to keep her family's thousands of acres and hundreds of animals in some sort of fruitful order.

At the far side, she could see the empty runway and the green hangar at its end. Most people in this part of the world drove pick-ups or sport utility vehicles to work. Misty's mother, Angela, depended on her Piper Cub, a small airplane she called *Hooter*. The plane's nickname came from the whooping noise that came from its engines when it was taxiing down the oiled runway in back of the corral. Hooter made it possible for her mother to criss-cross the country—and sometimes the world—buying and selling antiques.

Misty couldn't remember a time when her mother had been at the ranch for more than three weeks running. Angela coaxed the little plane into the air almost every Monday morning—or sometimes Sunday evening—and she generally managed to make a breathless return every Thursday or Friday afternoon. As a rule, she buried herself in her office for three or four hours, sorting and mumbling, barefoot and chewing on the ends of her long blond hair. When she emerged, it was as a butterfly from her cocoon— fluttering around her husband and her children with arms open wide and honey-colored hair swirling and circling behind her head like a comet. It was Thursday. Her mother would probably be returning to the nest.

Misty fished a hair-tie out of her pocket; the wind had changed, and her long hair was blowing into her face. As she lowered her head to roll the golden bun into the elastic, she noticed a large dark shape moving on the ground in the far distance—surrounded by clouds of dust and changing form like a flock of blackbirds. She fished her binoculars out of her saddle pack so she could look more closely at what she knew was a moving herd of horses—most certainly Mr. Lawford's renegade pack of Arabians.

Misty smiled faintly and squinted into the eastern horizon. Despite the dazzling glare of the mid-morning sun, she could see the Lawford place in the distance, nestled among massive old cottonwoods and tall, ungainly ponderosas. Strips of white fencing bordered the yard around the big old house that was ringed with country porches. The outbuildings were stacked behind, and the pond where she and her brother Ben loved to fish was just to the east—at the end of a row of plum trees. Mr. Lawford's wife had died five or so years before, so the place looked better from up here now than it did up close. The old man just wasn't interested in keeping up the flower gardens or seeing that the buildings were painted.

He welcomed company though. Misty and her brothers rode the horses or the four-wheelers over to the Lawford place at least once a month. He lived alone. His son was an eye surgeon in some big hospital in California, and George, the hired man who had helped Mr. Lawford run the place for the past ten years or so, left a while back to marry a school teacher in Lincoln.

Mr. Lawford's companions now were his two blue heelers and his horses—and nobody was sure how many horses he had. Some of their neighbors thought he had over 300—all Arabians. He let them run wild—and breed as they might. He was no longer interested in improving the breed—or in making money. He seemed content to stay on the place and keep time—and watch the horses—to just let things be.

She raised the high-powered binoculars her mother had brought for the family when she returned from one of her business trips to Germany. The glasses were so powerful that it always took a while to find the target she wanted to bring into focus. Ahh, there, she had them, a herd of perhaps 150 horses. She was stunned at how fast they were moving and how gracefully they seemed to weave among the hills. She had espied the horses many times from a distance, but whenever she or her brothers had tried to go near, the horses struck out in the opposite direction, pounding the ground resolutely as if to keep their secrets close.

The troop was usually led by an aristocratic gray stallion, one of Mr. Lawford's favorites. The old man's face got funny every time he looked at the gray or talked about him. The horse was fast and headstrong, and the other members of the herd had always moved behind him in ragged compliance. Today, however, the herd seemed to have another maestro, a leader that guided them with new power and purpose. Misty watched as the dark charger raced forward, his mane and tail flat out and blurred in the wind - his head high over a majestic crest, his strong back braced, and his slender legs in turn tucked under in mid-air as he routed the earth in rhythmic strides. The horse was an unusual liver chestnut—a kind of gray-red-black-brown. Misty held her breath. He had to be new. She had never seen him lead the herd before, and as she watched, she was sure he would never have fallen in as part of the pack. She scanned the herd to see the gray about two-thirds back and at the outside, running at an irregular gait as if injured.

As the distant rumble finally echoed its way up the bluff, her pony stirred, pawed the ground tentatively, and laid back his ears. Misty picked up the reins she had dropped when she took up the binoculars and steadied the pale buckskin under her saddle.

"It's all right, Cadaver. They're not coming up here." The gelding, named for its ashen color, large bones and impassive disposition, settled back into his stance but kept his ears up and his head raised.

5

A minute later the horse turned his big head to look below. Misty lowered the binoculars and looked down the path. It was her brother Ben. He was on Zelda, his leopard Appaloosa, a sturdy, dependable mare with a sparse main and almost no tail.

"Boy, the wind came up," he hollered when he was three big rocks from the top.

"So what else is new?" Misty turned her attention back to the herd below. "Hurry up!" she yelled. "I have something I want you to see."

Ben grunted as the horse climbed—as if it were the boy's and not the horse's effort that was taking them to the top of the bluff. His red hair scattered in short thatches below the White Sox baseball cap he wore, and he rode as he always did, with his head slightly to one side. He let the reins go slack as the striped hooves of the black and white mare picked expertly along the ragged path until she stepped up beside Cadaver.

Misty was still looking down the valley with the binoculars. "See the Lawford herd over there to the left?" Misty nodded sideways as she raised the glasses from her eyes.

Ben rose in his saddle and squinted. "Isn't that a new horse at the lead?" He had the best eyes of anyone Misty had ever known. He could spot hawks from more than half a mile away—and could even tell the difference between a red-tail and a Swainson's at that distance.

"Yep," said Misty. "Wanta look?" She handed the binoculars to Ben.

Ben crooned under his breath after he had focused the glasses on the herd. "Hot damn! Hot damn! Hot damn!" He whistled softly. "He may turn out to be ugly up close, but through these glasses, he's the biggest and best lookin' Arabian I ever saw."

Misty turned to look at her brother. "Do you think we can get closer?"

"We never were able to get close to the gray when he was in the lead."

"Yeah, but we didn't have these glasses before. If we could just get close enough to see him better through the glasses—." Misty took the binoculars from Ben and watched the herd slow as they approached a long pond, almost out of sight.

"Do you have anything t'eat? I wouldn't mind goin' down there, but it's gonna take a couple hours to ride down close enough. We have to go 'round the ravine, and it's almost ten now." Ben was rarely willing to do anything that meant he had to miss a meal.

"No, I don't have anything to eat." She paused. "But we could go down and pack a lunch, then take the horses in the trailer as far as Mr. Lawford's. We could ride the rest of the way."

"It'll take us an hour just to get home. You sure you're ready for such a long day? Don't you have a date or somethin'?" Ben wriggled his eyebrows a few times, then lowered his eyelids slyly. "You had a message from Slick McFarland."

Ben had called Misty's friend Danny McFarland, *Slick,* ever since Danny come to the house to pick up Misty wearing a suit and tie.

7

Misty gave Ben a lop-sided raspberry and turned her horse to start down the path.

"Cool it. His name is Danny, and yes, I still like him. He's a good shortstop; he's smart—and he doesn't pretend to know things he doesn't."

Ben leaned backward to shift the balance, so it would be easier for his horse to make her way down the slope. "But he can't even ride a horse—and he talks funny, like them cops on NYPD."

"He can too ride a horse. He just can't ride backwards like you, and most of Mom's East Coast friends talk like that. It's never bothered you before."

"Well, he came on kind a sudden—and I don't know—I guess I'm not used to you bein' able to talk like that to some other guy that's not in the family. You just seem so…" Ben paused to search for a word. "*Easy* with him."

"Well, I like him, and he can't help it if he comes from New Jersey. They ride different there, and from what he tells me, the horse country back east is beautiful. I'd like to see it sometime."

"Well, the way you're goin', you'll probably get the chance. When he looks at you with those baby blues, I get the feelin' he'd take you 'bout anywhere you'd ever wanta go."

"O.K., no more about Danny, O.K.? Let's just ride—or else I'll start in about Tru-u-udy Stanley." Misty sang out the girl's name with a heavy Southern swing.

Ben didn't reply. Trudy had been his girlfriend ever since they shared a desk in first grade at Blue Water School—one of the few one-room schoolhouses left on the prairies of Nebraska. Now they were both 15, and Trudy was a dazzling brunette with blue eyes and a wide smile, the flower of Goldenrod County Consolidated High School, the school they all attended after eighth grade. It had been a struggle for Ben to watch Trudy attend dances and school events with an assortment of upperclassmen. He gritted his teeth and rode the rest of way in silence.

At the base of the bluff, they pushed their mounts toward home. They circled the knife-like blades of the yuccas and galloped through the feathery grasses. They opened the gates so they could ride through horse pastures that were fenced securely with angular split-rails, six feet high—or were bordered by heavy cable strung on sturdy poles. They rode across cattle pastures that ran on for miles with nothing but rag-tag barbed wire to close them in from the roads. Here and there, far from the lakes, they went past the whirling windmills that sucked water into the stock tanks.

In less than an hour, they could see the wrought iron *Diamond W* that hung over the entrance to their ranch.

Chapter Two

They worked fast. In half an hour, they had the horses loaded; there was a lunch in a box on the front seat of the big red four-wheel-drive pick-up, and they were bumping down the road.

Misty was driving. They had to go off property and along a county road for five miles of the 10-mile trip to Lawford's ranch, and at 17 she had a driver's license. Not quite 15, Ben and Tony had permits that licensed them to drive only to school and school events.

Once they left the county road, Ben asked, "How big is the Lawford place, anyway?"

"I don't know—20,000 acres or so," Misty replied. "I know it's not as big as ours. It's shaped funny; I saw an aerial photograph once. It looks kind of like a mushroom."

"What kinda mushroom?"

"Oh, you know—the kind you buy in those little boxes in the grocery store."

"You mean the ones Mom stuffs with that awful crab stuff."

"Those stuffed mushrooms are delicious and you know it." Misty reached for a sandwich.

"So on the map, is the mushroom right side up, with the big part on the top—to the north?" Ben swallowed.

"Well, yeah, but it's a little skewed to the right, like when you rotate a picture just a little bit on the computer." Misty turned to cut onto the one-track road that led to the Lawford ranch.

"We'd better stop and tell Mr. Lawford what we're doin' before we go look at the horses," Ben said with a mouthful of ham sandwich.

"Yeah, we should," Misty agreed. "I'm sure he wouldn't care, but I'd feel better if he knew we were on his place."

It took only 15 minutes before they were skirting along the winding gravel lane toward Mr. Lawford's big white house. Once in front, Ben put his can of apple juice in the cup holder of the truck and climbed down.

"Don't see his pickup," he said, then shrugged and walked toward the house. He paused only briefly to kneel and pet the two blue heelers that barked then wagged their tales in recognition. As they followed, he sauntered up the steps and across the porch on the front of the house, then knocked loudly on the front door.

"There's a doorbell!" Misty yelled out her window.

Ben scowled and raised his thumb to the button on the left side of the screen door. He leaned there while he counted to 10. His efforts were greeted only by the sound of the wind pushing dry leaves across the gray painted floor of the planked porch and into the corner under the porch swing. He turned back to the truck.

"Doesn't look like he's home," Ben said as he climbed up to his seat.

"Should we go in to the pasture anyway?" asked Misty.

"Let's leave him a note," Ben suggested. "That way if he comes home and sees the trailer, he'll know what's goin' on."

Misty nodded. "Find some paper."

Ben opened the glove compartment and rifled through its contents. He finally retrieved a dirty envelope with *Goldenrod County Consolidated High School* in the upper left-hand corner and their brother's name on the front.

"Oh gross, it's one of Tony's old report cards." Ben slid the card from the envelope, studied it, and groaned. "Perfect as always. Listen to this—'Tony is my best student. I recommend he take Advanced Calculus next semester. I feel he is wasting his time with the required math courses.'" He threw the card back in the glove compartment and pulled a ball-point pen from beside it. "If I ever got a report card like that, I'd blow it up and make a bumper sticker out of it."

"You and Tony just have different talents, that's all." Misty smiled. "How can two boys, twins, who look so much alike be so different?" She used a husky, eastern voice, imitating her mother.

Ben wrote on the envelope. "How's this? Mr. Lawford: Misty and I are riding in your pasture, hoping to get a closer look at your new stallion. We should be back here between three and four o'clock. Signed Ben West."

"That should do it."

After Ben stuck the note at the edge of the screen in the door on the porch and returned to the truck, Misty backed the pick-up and trailer into an empty place beside the barn. They guided their horses, which were still saddled from the morning ride, out of the trailer.

They rode west and south toward the spot where they had seen the herd earlier that day. When they reached the long pond, the ground around it was loose and dimpled from all of the hooves that had trampled there that morning, but they couldn't hear or see the horses.

"Looks like they headed west. Let's try over by the canyon," Ben suggested after examining the horses' tracks.

They turned their horses and traveled straight west until they reached a deep gorge that ran for over a mile under the shadow of tall cedars and juniper trees. They looked down along the stream in the ravine. There was no sign of the herd.

"Well, what now?" Misty asked.

"Let's go up on that hill and just listen." Ben turned the appaloosa to the south toward a high dune in the distance. Once on top of the hill, they dismounted and tied their mounts to the warty bark of a small hackberry tree.

Ben sat down on a large rock and took off his hat. Misty knew that she had to remain as still as possible while he listened. For some time he didn't move, then slowly he turned himself onto the ground, picked small rocks off a flat surface, took a red bandanna out of his pocket, laid it on the ground, and then put his ear down to the earth. In a few minutes, he arose and brushed off the side of his hair that had lain in the dust. He nodded to the west. "They're over there—about five miles I'd guess." He frowned. "It's funny. It sounds like they're just runnin' back and forth."

"Why would they do that?"

13

"Don't know. Let's go, Zelda." He swung his leg over his saddle.

They rode for almost quarter of an hour before Ben spurred Zelda to the top of a hill and with the binoculars finally spotted the horses in the distance. They were a black wisp on a flat stretch between two large rock formations both Misty and Ben knew well. The smaller one was about 50-feet high and was called "Apple Rock" because the wind had shaped the sandstone into a smooth, round ball that grew larger toward the top and had an elongated rocky plate on one side that looked like a leaf. The larger one was called "Picnic Rock" because there were rocks that climbed almost like stairs on one side, and at the west side of the flat table-like top, there was a wall that tapered down and inward from about nine feet to six feet. Before Mrs. Lawford's death, the Lawfords had hosted summer picnics for their neighbors on this shaded plateau. Families would bring baskets of food and climb to the top to feast under the shelter of the wall.

Ben looked through the binoculars for a long time. Finally he lowered them and said so softly that Misty could barely hear, "I can't figure out what they're doin'. They just go back and forth between Apple and Picnic." He raised the glasses up to look again, then shook his head.

"Let's ride," He muttered, "but as we get close we have to ride gentle, so they don't hear us."

Misty and Ben trotted the horses for about half an hour before they reached a place where they could climb to a high spot and look again. This time they could see the horses below them, still running back and forth between the rocks, following the big stallion as they had this morning. Misty took the binoculars.

"I think I see something." She looked for a long time, then handed the glasses to Ben. "What's that to the right of the herd?"

Ben frowned as he looked through the glasses. "It looks like a wagon—no, maybe it's one of those golf carts that's been rigged up with a little wagon in back—like they have at the Sandhills Golf Course." He paused. "No, it's too big for one of those golf carts. Let's get closer." He didn't hesitate, but rode off the knoll at full speed. Misty followed, not sure they shouldn't be more cautious.

They urged their horses to full gallop. When they were about a half-mile from the herd, the horses turned and came toward them. Ben and Misty changed direction, trying to come up on their far side. They turned to a small, slanting butte, keeping their heads down in their jackets to avoid the dirt that was kicked up in clouds under the horses' hooves. They reined up behind a thick stand of junipers and watched the herd stampede around them, the powerful new stallion a dark pounding shadow in the dust.

"He's beautiful," shouted Misty through the rumble of the horses' passing.

"Sure is. I never thought we'd get this close," hooted Ben. "Oh, oh, look back there. No wonder they're runnin'."

Misty turned to peer through the trees and the dust. Two big machines—Humvees painted in dull army green—were coming up the other side of the herd with their big engines gunned to top speed. Ben and Misty watched as the drivers of the big broad "Hummers" hunkered in behind their steering wheels, slouched into their camouflage jackets. The giant square machines with the mammoth tires swerved and drove toward the horses as if to ram them, then they would back off, their engines racing. One of the vehicles thrust its way into the middle of the herd then up the opposite side of the pack, narrowing the pass through which the horses could run and causing them to jolt and kick each other.

Misty and Ben shook their heads in anger; it was too noisy to talk. When the Humvee's had passed, the two guided their horses down the hill behind a tree row fronted by irregular cedars and backed up by towering willows. They dismounted.

"Well?" asked Misty when they flopped down side by side just behind the hill, and the noise of the horses and their pursuers was in the distance.

"I don't know. I'm not ready to ask these guys what they're doin'. I have one rule of thumb. Never mix in the business of a guy wearin' military gear— even if he bought it at Wal-Mart." Ben's words were flip, but his tone was serious.

"I don't know 'em, d'you?" Misty wiped the dirt from her eyes.

"Not only do I not know 'em, I've never even heard of anyone around here who has a Humvee," said Ben. "What could they be tryin' to do?"

"Beats me. Do you have your cell phone?" asked Misty.

"Nah, I didn't bring it, 'cause we have the bag phone in the truck." Ben was referring to a cellular telephone with extra wattage; they kept it in the pickup that pulled the horse trailer. "Should we try t'circle around in the other direction t'get to the house?"

"Let's let 'em get gone a little further," said Misty. She drew a few deep breaths, then said, "Isn't that stallion something? I feel as though I'm in some sort of spell whenever I watch him."

"Yep, he's somethin'," Ben replied. "He sort a' shimmers, even in the dust. Maybe those guys are tryin' to catch *him*."

"Get down, they're comin' back." They could hear the roar of the motors grow louder as the Humvee's raced toward the valley just below. She climbed the hill and peered down to see the two vehicles, side-by-side going past them in the opposite direction from where the horses had fled. "Do you think torturing horses is their idea of fun? What in the world were they doing?"

"Good thing they didn't look back," rumbled Ben. "Wonder where they came from." The Humvee's had disappeared over the hill beyond Apple Rock. He stood up and raised the glasses to find the horses. They were running at a steadfast pace across the flat prairie in the opposite direction.

"What do we call him?" Ben asked after a while.

Misty knew he was referring to the new stallion. She paused before replying, thinking of the elegant, yet powerful animal. Like most Arabians, his head was small with a dish face and wide forehead, and his back was short, but he was taller than most of his breed, probably almost 16 hands. He had hurled forward gracefully, calmly and at thunderous speed, leading the herd away from the menacing machines.

"I'm sure he already has a name," she said finally as she untied her horse, "but if I were going to name him, I'd call him Mirage." She swung her leg over Cadaver's back, settled in the saddle and added, "He's like a ghost from some other world; it was almost mystical when he came out of the dust. He's like no horse I've ever seen."

Ben grunted in agreement, rose to mount his horse and led her away in a gallop.

Misty and Ben slowed their horses as they got closer to Lawford's. The same thought was circling through both their minds: *what if the drivers of the Humvees were also on their way to the Lawford ranch?* They reined in as they approached the Lawford ranch buildings, opened the gate from the pasture carefully, and walked toward a machine shed. Behind the shed, they tied their horses and crept up slowly along the fence of the barnyard until they could see their pickup and trailer. Everything seemed just as they left it. Mr. Lawford's big green pickup was still missing from its usual place at the side of the house, the dogs were sleeping by the back steps, and only the wind broke the silence as it moaned over the hayrack at the side of the metal building.

"Let's go home," said Misty. Quickly they retrieved their horses and loaded them into the trailer, stopping only briefly to wipe the tired animals with a towel where they were sweaty from running. In just a few minutes their truck and trailer were leaving a fog of dust behind them.

"Call Dad," Misty said as she guided the big red 350 along the washboard gravel road.

Ben reached for the handset of the telephone. "Funny," he said as he examined the LCD screen on the handset of the telephone. "It seems dead."

He reached down to shake the adapter plug and make sure it was inserted into the receptacle on the dash that gave it power. "Must be somethin' wrong. It should run on the batteries even if it's not plugged in." Slowly he ran the cord to the handset through his hands.

"Oops, you're not going to like this," Ben said with a croaky voice. "The cord's been cut.

Chapter Three

Misty swallowed hard and pressed her boot to the accelerator—driving as fast as the bumpy, sandy road and the heavy load she was towing would allow. Ben kept his eyes ahead, around and behind them, looking for any sight of someone following or watching.

Once they came to the top of the hill where they could see the entrance to the Diamond W, they leaned back in their seats in relief. Misty's eyes stung and her muscles ached from holding the steering wheel so fiercely. She blinked, wiggled her fingers and cleared her throat, so Ben wouldn't know she had been so scared.

Her brother looked to the back, to the trailer, hoping the horses were all right. He could see Cadaver; the tall gelding seemed a bit shaken by the bumpy ride and was nodding his head, his ears back in agitation. He seemed fine otherwise, though.

As they pulled into the yard, they saw an old gray Range Rover parked in front of the house.

"Mom's home," Ben said needlessly.

"Yep," Misty muttered. "I don't think we should tell her about the Humvee thing and the bag phone until we get Dad's take on all this. She'll lock us up somewhere."

"Amen," said Ben. He took a deep breath and prepared himself to appear to be as calm as possible. Maybe it was because his mother was away from home so much. She just came undone when she caught a clue that her children were at any kind of risk. He remembered the last fit she had when she discovered they were riding out at night to find coyotes.

Ben could imagine exactly what she would say. "That's it, Hank," slowly, sadly, very different from her usual mercurial patter. BIG SIGH, PAUSE. "You give these kids entirely too much freedom. When these children go out wandering in these hills, you or Charlie or one of the men have to go along—or maybe I'll just have to start working from home all the time, so I can go with them. I just can't be away if I have to worry about what red-neck is going to come at them with some souped-up tractor."

It would go on. She would say the same thing in different words—in a husky, near-tears voice that would leave everyone in the room entirely sympathetic and his father speechless and miserable. It was likely that about two hours later, after some discussion of the situation, she would recant, and allow that her children were very resourceful and clever people who could probably handle most any predicament, but both Ben and Misty had learned delay tactics to avoid the preliminary, gut-wrenching scene.

"I'll go in and tell 'em we're home, and then I'll be out to help you put the horses away," said Ben.

"O.K.," said Misty as she pulled up on the other side of the lilac bush that guarded the front of the house. "What if they tried t'call us? Why didn't we answer?"

"Simple truth," Ben replied as he opened the door. "The cell phone didn't ring while we were in the pickup." He slammed it shut. "I'll be out t'the barn in a minute." Misty pulled away as her brother leaped up the back steps.

"Anybody home?" he shouted as he pushed into the house. Once inside he tried again. "Hey, anybody around?"

"In here." His mother's voice came from the back of the house where his father's office was located. Quickly, he took off his boots, so he wouldn't take the chance of losing time hearing a lecture from Claire about dust and gravel on the polished oak floor. He socks were damp. Funny, he didn't know fear made your feet sweat.

As he approached the half-open door to the office, he heard his father mutter, "The last time I heard of any real problems out here was during the late 70's—and that turned out to be some no-goods from around Casper." His father looked quickly at Ben as he came through the door then turned his attention back to Ben's mother who was perched on the corner of the big oak desk.

"Jim McAndrews is pretty hot," he continued, "specially since the sheriff won't even take the time to come out and look—won't even file a report. Says the calves will probably come wanderin' up one of these days. But I know Jim, and if he says those cows are nowhere on his land, they just aren't there." Hank West tapped his pen on his desk in an offbeat rhythm. He was leaning back in his desk chair, squinting and frowning at Ben's mother as he went on in his deep voice that had an unusual edge.

"Steve Griese's missin' 15 head, and Larry Lopez is missin' 10. Seems to me that would be enough to get the attention of the law, but then, maybe I don't know the whole story." Ben's father leaned forward, grabbed a tissue and blew his nose. "Damned allergies."

Angela West murmured agreement, then turned her attention to the dusty redhead in front of them. She rose to give him a hug, and Ben embraced her familiar compact body. She was still dressed in her flying uniform: a purple sweat-suit and high-top running shoes. He caught a faint smell of diesel fuel but it was covered by his mother's spicy scent that always made him think of the big department stores in Denver where you could buy expensive colognes and silk pajamas.

"Take off your hat, you're in the house." Ben's mom smiled.

Ben folded his hat from his head, stuck it in his back pocket, and ran his hand over his shaggy hair.

"Claire said you kids went over to the Lawford place," said his father. "Did you see John?"

"Yea, we just got back, but Mr. Lawford wasn't there."

Hank West frowned at the answer. Ben hesitated, then said, "But we saw his new Arabian."

Ben's father frowned. "You been chasin' those horses?"

"No, Dad, of course not. We spotted the herd from up on the bluff, then went over t'where we could get a good look at 'em through the glasses. The horse leadin' the herd now is bigger'n any Arabian I ever heard of—and kind of a dark chestnut. Powerful horse."

"Think he's new, huh?" asked his father.

"Misty's sure he is." Ben turned away to discourage questions. "I gotta go now and help her put away the horses. We'll be back in as soon as we're done." Ben looked back at his mother. "What time's supper?"

"You mean *dinner*," she grinned. Angela had grown up in a brownstone in southern Philadelphia and spent most of her workweek in one city or another around the world. She loved the plains of western Nebraska and was devoted to the man behind the desk, but she drew the line at calling the evening meal *supper*.

She looked at her watch. "Well, I've got at least three hours of bookwork. I stopped in the kitchen, and Claire was making chicken pot pies. Wouldn't think it would matter when we put them in the oven. Can you have a snack, then we can all sit down around eight? Tony should be home by then."

"Did y'hear from him? Did they win?" Goldenrod had been closed for teachers' meetings this week, and Tony was part of a math team that, since Tuesday, had been at Ponderosa State College 100 miles to the north. The competition was called "Mathathletics," and if they won, they would bring home a modest silver trophy for the school that seemed to Ben small reward for having spent evenings and weekends during the last two months challenging each other with improbable puzzles and thinking up extra homework. But it was important to Tony, and Ben was Tony's twin, so it was important to Ben—and his parents might have guessed something was off if he hadn't asked.

"He called me on the cell just a few minutes ago," said Angela. "They were waiting for the results. He didn't sound very optimistic. Seems they didn't spend enough time on the slide rule."

Ben wanted to ask, "What's a slide rule?" but worse he wanted to get back to help Misty and didn't want his parents to ask any more questions. He grunted something he hoped would sound like he understood, then said, "Gotta go help with the horses. See you at *dinner*." He grinned, turned quickly from the room and jogged down the hall toward his boots.

Misty had the horses unloaded and was in the back stall working on the buckle of Cadaver's saddle when Ben came into the barn eating something wrapped in gold foil. "Want one?" He fanned out three more candy bars.

"Not right now," she said as she slid the saddle and blanket from the horses back. "What did they say?"

"Not much. Seems Mr. McAndrews and some other guys lost some cattle, and Dad had that on his mind. He asked if we'd seen Mr. Lawford." Ben stuck the candy bars under his hat and went to the next stall where Zelda was standing patiently, waiting for Ben to take off her gear. Gently he squeezed himself into the crack on the horse's left side, then pushed her forward, so he could hold the reins and buckle the halter strap around her neck. He fastened the halter to the gate, so she wouldn't move around while he worked.

His mind was busy with the image of the Arabian running his herd from the brutish machines, and he removed the horse's tack without a conscious thought

25

as to what he was doing. First he unbuckled the noseband and throatlatch, then gently slid the headstall over her ears and removed the bridle. He adjusted the halter, so the horse was still tethered to the gate, and he worked carefully, because Zelda had been known to try to pin him against the stall when she was impatient and hungry. After he untied the cinch knot and tucked the straps into the dee ring, he worked himself over to her spotted right side where he threw the cinch over the seat of the saddle and looped the right stirrup over the saddle horn. He ducked quickly under the pony to get back to her left side. As he crawled through he noticed a dusting of yellow powder on the back of her left hoof. With one hand on the barrel of her stomach, he leaned down to rub a bit of the powder on his finger. He smelled it. Nothing hit his nose—probably something from the trailer. He wiped the dust on his jeans and in one slow motion, lifted the blanket and saddle off Zelda's back.

He stood for a few minutes then, lost in thought, trying to come up with a logical answer for why anyone would cut their cell phone cord—until he heard Misty flip the latch on Cadaver's stall. Ben patted Zelda quietly, unhooked her halter rope from the gate and followed Misty out of the barn. The horses had cooled down during their ride in the trailer, but Misty and her brother led them around the barnyard for a few minutes anyway, not allowing them to eat or drink until they were satisfied the horses were no longer sweaty.

After they led the horses back to the barn, they groomed them in silence. In a few minutes, they heard their father's footsteps in the gravel at the entrance, and soon Hank West had settled himself on a tree stump that sat under the tack board outside the stalls.

"I was lookin' out my office window and saw you when you were comin' down the road. What was goin' on that you thought you had to raise that much dust?" His voice was quiet and serious.

Misty pulled herself from behind Cadaver's long neck, thankful that her father trusted them and was slow to place blame. "We were scared," she said and sat on a bail of straw beside him to relate what had happened that afternoon.

"I don't think you two ought go over there alone 'til we find out what's goin' on," said Hank when she had finished. "You have anything to add, Ben? Never heard you be this quiet."

Ben shook his head and took another chocolate bar from under his cap. Another thing he had discovered about fear: it made him very hungry.

"I tried to call John before I left the house. He's still not home. Never heard of him lettin' strangers on his land when he or one of his hands wasn't along." He paused, removed his hat, and rubbed his forehead with the back of his hard, brown hand. "You sure you never saw those guys before?"

Ben looked at Misty. They both shook their heads.

"We couldn't really see 'em very well because of the glasses and those funny army hats," said Ben, "but I think I would have known if it was somebody from around here."

"Well, let's not tell your mother about all this just yet." He grinned on one side of his face. "I guess you

27

two figured that out." After a while, he added, "I suppose I should call the sheriff, but a fat lot of good that'd probably do—he won't even come out to file a report on thirty-forty thousand dollars worth a missin' calves."

He sat in silence for a few minutes while Misty went to hang up Cadaver's saddle and Ben unwrapped the last of his candy, a marshmallow nut bar. Then Hank stood and set his big black hat on the back of his head.

"Well, let's let things be for tonight. I'll call later and see if John's home yet. If he isn't, I'll call around in town to see if anybody knows where he might be. Wouldn't have gone too far without tellin' us." As he stepped out of the barn, he added, "If I don't talk to him by in the morning, we'll go over there and see if we can find out what's been goin' on. You two go feed the cattle. You'll have to do Tony's share too."

When he was half-way out of the barn, he shouted over his shoulder, "Oh, by the way, I forgot—Tony's team came in second. Some hotshot bunch from the school by Offut Air Force Base beat 'em out."

Ben and Misty frowned. They hoped this wasn't a big deal for Tony. Whenever Tony didn't come out on top, he always put up a brave and modest face to the world, but his brother and sister sometimes had to listen for days or weeks as he dribbled on about what he could have or should have done. Their worst experience so far had been when he lost the state spelling bee two years ago. He agonized for days about how he had carelessly omitted one of the "g's" in the word *aggrandizement*. Misty and Ben had finally shut him up by making him spell each morning as they rode to school; they gave him every word in the dictionary and were both very grateful when he won the contest the next year. But since they knew nothing about algorithms and calculus, both of them were wondering what they were going to do if they had to help Tony cope with this new blip in his almost-perfect scholastic history.

"Hey, he's a big boy now. He's got to learn he's not perfect," said Misty.

"We've said that before," said Ben. "But y'have t'admit, he is pretty perfect."

"Yeah, it's scary." Neither of them was jealous of Tony. Mostly, everyone on the ranch—in fact, mostly everyone in the whole county—was just amazed by him. He was an athlete, a musician, an artist, a linguist, an amateur scientist, a writer, a comedian, and a computer hacker. The only things he had shown little interest in had to do with his father's business. He was good with the horses, but had no real interest in the animals in general. He considered his father's horses and range-fed herds of beautiful, white Charolais cattle a somewhat entertaining, but not very effective, way of making money.

As they were walking to the hay barn to get the feed for the cattle, Misty said, "I can't wait to tell Tony about what happened today. Do you s'pose those Humvee's have anything to do with the cattle that'r missing?'

"Who knows," Ben shrugged. "Seems like overkill though. You could pick up cows with a cattle truck and a forkful a'hay. Why would you wanta bring in noisy army equipment?"

"I don't think those guys thought anyone else was around. Most people don't consider how far any kinda noise travels around here." Misty paused, then added, "And I can't imagine anyone not from cattle country stealin' cattle. It would have to be someone that has somewhere to sell 'em—and someone who knows how to get around the branding and the tags."

"Well, maybe those yearlings are just playin' hide and seek. People have lost cattle before and then found 'em in a blowout somewhere. I'm more worried about those guys chasin' the Arabians." Ben grabbed a pitchfork and turned into the hay barn.

"Probably just out for a joy ride," Misty said contemptuously. "That's just so sick—scarin' animals just for the fun of it.

Chapter Four

"Hey Tony, wanta play?" Joe Griese waved a pack of poker cards in Tony's face.

"Nah, not right now," Tony growled. "Besides, I'd probably end up with that fancy belt buckle your dad gave you for your birthday."

Joe looked down proudly at the large silver medallion with a raised buffalo in the center. It connected a carved leather belt that was looped by faded Levi's. "You wish!" he grinned and lurched to the back of the school bus.

Tony leaned his head against the cold glass of the window and closed his eyes. What a long day—and it'd be another hour before they would get back to the school—and another half an hour or so after that before he got home. He couldn't wait to start the 10-year-old green Bronco that was his "school car" and drive home to the Diamond W.

He tried to take shallow breaths, so the smell in the bus wasn't so suffocating. He was used to cow pee and horse manure; and when they rode home from basketball or football games, sometimes it was pretty sweaty and funky, but the muggy fog of phony sweetness that slunk into his nose now was making his stomach roll. It was an overpowering fusion of bubble gum, musky perfumes, spicy deodorants, flowery hair treatments, and fruity lotions—and it wasn't just the girls. Jimmy Hendren was sitting to his right, banging his head rhythmically against the back of the seat in front of him—presumably to the tune in his earphones—and some sort of too-sweet bouquet was wafting from his spiky hair.

Tony shifted in his seat and buried his nose in the jacket that was draped around the front of his shoulders and over his crossed arms. He knew his senses were skewed because he was in a bad mood. It had happened before. But his team had come so close—would have won if they had just given Jim and Amy some more time on the slide rule. And he knew he shouldn't expect to win every time—but why not? If it was *possible*? And this had been completely within possibility. He checked himself again, insistently. "Lighten up! Chill!" He told himself.

He could see Lono in her seat three rows ahead, facing firmly away, listening deliberately to something Mattie Gleason was saying from across the aisle. Lono had been his friend, then his girlfriend, ever since they met at the horse show at the county fair three years ago when they were not quite twelve years old. Her name was Lori Nolde. Lono was her nickname, given to her by local radio announcers who covered her trials and triumphs in barrel racing.

Normally, she would be sitting next to him, holding his hand, playing with his fingers, discussing the high and low points of each of their competitions— and the various small dramas involved: his in math, hers in history. This evening, however, when boarding the bus, she had seen him slumped in the corner of his seat and had walked right past the seat beside him. She knew he was sulking because his team didn't win the trophy, and she had no time for what she saw as a poor loser.

One of the boys in front of Tony stuck his head through the space between the seats. "Hey, Tony, d'ya hear about the blind man who had a yellow leg?" When Tony didn't answer, he said, "He had a blind dog."

Tony smiled, but the boys were disappointed and turned back and didn't offer any more jokes. They had been raising their heads over the seats, looking back for some time, to see if Tony didn't want to enter in as they traded stories. Tony knew more jokes and told them better than anyone in the school. Once, on the way back from a field trip to Kearney, 100 miles away, Tony had told jokes from memory for the entire two hours.

Slinking back under his coat, he closed his ears to the "and then this duck walked into the bar…" and checked his glow-in-the-dark watch: 5:45. He should be home by quarter to eight at the latest. He retrieved a cell phone from his jacket pocket and pressed one of the memory buttons.

"Ho." It was his brother Ben.

"Whad ya have for supper?" Tony mumbled.

"*Dinner*, Mom's home. We didn't eat yet, we're waitin' for you," Ben said, then he added sarcastically, "Sounds like you're in a good mood."

"I'm tryin' to be," Tony muttered. "O.K. I should be there in about an hour or so…"

"Wait'll ya hear what we did today," Ben broke in. "Me an' Misty'll tell you about it after we eat."

"Tell me now," said Tony.

"Well, we went over to Lawford's place. Saw his new Arabian. You wouldn't believe what happened.

33

"Just as..." crack, snap, silence "and then Misty..." crack, snap "loud..." snap, silence "running like crazy..." Ben's words were covered then with a buzz of loud static which cut away to nothing. Tony looked outside and saw the electrical transformers—enormous dual pillars joined with braces in the middle that marched across the plains at perfect intervals—like an army of alien soldiers. Tony knew they stretched on for miles, and there was no use in trying to talk until they got back into clear air. Tony flicked the phone closed, leaned back and closed his eyes. He'd rather hear the story from both of them anyway.

He was feeling better by the time he turned the Bronco off the county road at Stoop's Corner. Stoop's was a leftover filling station that had been closed ever since Tony could remember and had been part of his family's ranch since his father had paid the back taxes and incorporated it into his holdings before Tony was born. It marked the turnoff to the Diamond W.

The windows of the old gas station were boarded up, the stucco had cracked off in spots, and ragged weeds thrived in the cracks of the wide cement driveway. Its companion, an old two-story grain storage building loomed just behind and to the side. Each time Tony passed it, he wondered that the top of the storage building hadn't collapsed, but it stood, peeling but stalwart, with twin cupolas leaning inward at each end or the roof.

Every year when things got slow, his father would say, "Well this might be the time to tear down Stoop's Corner." But something would happen that took up his attention, and the buildings at Stoop's still stood, relics from a simpler time. Everything north and west of Stoops for over 50 square miles belonged to Tony's family, and he knew the road so well, he was sure he could drive the five miles home even if he were blind.

It was a clear night with only a shred of a moon; one of the nights when he could see all the stars and wonder at how black it was beneath them. The broad beams from the Bronco's headlights made the only light, and as he drove, the low rumble of the motor provided a comforting backdrop for the music on Nebraska Public Radio. It was Beethoven's First Concerto for Violin—one of his favorites. Misty liked it too. If Ben had been with him, he probably would have turned to one of his rap CD's, or some jazz, or maybe some rock. Ben didn't like any kind of music that didn't have a beat that vibrated the seats of the car. But Ben wasn't along, and Tony was glad he was alone.

He had started feeling better after he gathered with the other members of his team beside the empty school bus. Lono had been glaring at him from where she was standing, waiting for her ride, and he had forced himself to approach Dave, Jim and Amy who were standing with Mr. Jakes.

Ed Jakes, their laid-back, jean-clad sponsor, a science instructor turned math teacher because the school couldn't lure one to Goldenrod, had been speaking to the group. "Speaking mathematically and metaphorically," he had said good-naturedly, "the odds of our having four students who can compete at this level are about the same as my beating Tiger Woods at golf. What you've done gets statewide attention for our school. Way to go guys." He shook hands with each of them, then smoothed his mustache with his forefingers, thinking privately that they were all so grown up, so poised. He was sure they were more mature than he had been at 22—when he had started his teaching career in an Omaha middle school six years earlier.

"Yeah, we did O.K," Tony forced himself to say. "Here we were—from a little school in the part of the state that has almost no people." There were only 258 students in Goldenrod, the junior high and high school combined. "And we beat out teams from schools with 800 or 1,000 kids in just one class." Saying it seemed to make it true.

The other kids had mumbled agreement or disagreement. It was difficult to tell. Tony knew they knew how easily they could have won.

"See ya Monday." Mr. Jakes had walked toward his van, and with relief, Tony had waved at Lono and loped toward the Bronco.

Four miles from home. One, then another, and another jackrabbit crossed 20 or 30 feet ahead in the glare of his headlights. He never got used to how big they were; one rabbit was taller than the middle wire in the fence; his ears were as tall as his body. Tony watched the big-footed hares bounce among the sage, then braked slightly as he thought he saw something else at the edge of the shaft of his headlights. He released the gas pedal, slowed the motor, then braked to a stop. Shifting into reverse, he gunned the Bronco back up the road. About four car-lengths back and some 20 feet off the road, he found it. As he drove up beside it, the ugly turkey vultures that were squatting to the side flew back up into the night. He retrieved a million-candlepower lamp from the assortment of coats and gadgets in the back, got out of the Bronco, leaned over the hood and shined the lamp on what he thought had looked like an animal of some sort. It was. The black and white, slightly furry hide of a close-to-yearling calf glistened in the bright light. Tony recognized it immediately as one of Jimmy McAndrews' Dutch Belteds. Tony and his brother and sister had always called them "oreo cows" because they were all black with only a wide white stripe running around their middles and along their stomachs. This one probably weighed in at around 700 pounds.

Tony walked with the beam of the lamp to where the calf lay. He wiggled the black legs. They were stiff, but one of them stuck slightly sideways, probably broken. The neck was taut and angled upward. The calf was dead, of course. Tony kneeled down to examine the animal's ear; it had been sliced inward from the outside edge, and the steer's identification tag had been removed. Must have been in a hurry. Tony checked for a brand. None on this side. Judging from how stiff the big animal was, he had to have been dead for three or four hours, but probably not more than eight. He frowned at a bit of yellow powder on his finger. He rubbed it with his thumb, wiped it on his pants, then he took his cell phone from his pocket and pressed the memory key for home.

"Yup," came his father's voice.

"I'm about four miles from home. I found a dead calf just off the road—one of Jimmy M's Dutch Belted almost-yearlings," Tony said.

"I'll be damned," Hank West said after a slight pause. "How dead?"

"I'd say a few hours," said Tony.

Hank cleared his throat, then decided, "Stay there. Jimmy's not home; he and Lucy went to Denver. Be back late tonight. Ben and me'll come, and we'll get it into the truck. D'you have a chain?"

"I have the log chain we used to drag those telephone poles last week," Tony answered. "Don't have any plastic though. Probably wanna keep this fella sealed up."

"We'll bring a tarp—be there shortly. We'll be drivin' the brown diesel—might need the winch and overhead spot." His father paused. "You get back in the Bronco, kill the lights, and lock the doors. Don't stick around if someone besides us comes your way. This has been a strange day." The line went dead.

Chapter Five

It was Misty, not Ben, who was sitting on the passenger side of the truck when his father pulled up beside Tony and rolled down the window.

"You O.K.?" asked Tony's father as he turned the spot on the dead calf.

"Just hungry," said Tony.

Hank opened the door and jumped from the truck. Misty rummaged through the pockets of her jacket, found a half-eaten bag of trail mix, and tossed it to her brother.

"Get that log chain," said their father as he started over to examine the calf.

"I got it right here." Tony gestured to the seat beside him.

Holding his snack with his teeth, Tony opened the door, scooped up the heavy chain, and slid out of the car with a grunt. He walked over to the calf and dropped the heavy load at its feet. He unzipped the top of the package of trail mix, poured some of the contents in his mouth and chewed while Misty and his father poked and prodded at the dead animal. They were wearing latex gloves. Hank had trouble with his thumbs cracking when the weather got cold, so he usually carried a package of gloves in the front pocket of the padded overalls he was wearing. Tony wasn't surprised his father thought it sensible to protect their skin from whatever had killed the calf and hoped he hadn't picked up anything when he had touched the animal earlier. But Tony had only touched his legs.

He remembered the yellow powder he had had on his thumb, but that was probably not worth mentioning. Besides he didn't want his father to know he'd touched the dead animal without protection.

"Doesn't look like he was sick, that's for sure," said Misty. "Other than the broken leg and a broken neck, that is. Weird about the ear tag."

"Not if the calf was stolen," said her father.

"Who'd be dumb enough to steal an oreo cow? Any brand inspector or sale barn would I.D. it in a minute," she came back. "There can't be over 50 oreos in the entire state."

"If that many," said Hank.

"Where's Ben?" Tony asked as he examined the bag for more trail mix, found none, crumpled the package in his hand and lobbed it through the open window of the truck.

"Your mom had him puttin' stuff on the computer," said his father. "Thought it best to let 'em be. Told 'em we were goin' to pick up a lost calf." His father grunted as he wrapped the heavy chain around the calf's hind legs. "Ordinarily I'd leave this striped so and so here, but I wouldn't want the scavengers to destroy any evidence as to how he mighta been killed."

They worked as a team for twenty minutes before they had the other end of the chain on the truck's winch and could lift the heavy calf into the air and onto the opaque plastic sheet they had spread on the bed of the truck. Once there, they gathered the plastic at each corner and folded it over the black and white body, then fastened it with duct tape.

"Let's go," said Hank. "Misty, why don't you ride home with Tony? I think I'll take this fella over to Jimmy's."

Misty wrinkled her face at her father. "Mom's goin' ta be pretty mad if you're not there for dinner."

"Yeah, I spose yer right, and besides I'm hungry. I'll take it over in the morning. Tony, give me your cell, and I'll leave him a message on the way home."

Tony tossed the telephone to his father.

Misty started toward the Bronco. "I'll ride with Tony anyway. Ben said he got cut off when he was telling him about what happened today. I can fill him in."

"O.K." Hank started toward the truck, then turned back. "Hey, Tony, I heard you guys took second. That's quite a deal. Made me proud. You can tell us about it at supper."

"*Dinner*. Mom's home," Tony's lips tilted up in a small smile, then he growled, "We shoulda got first."

After Tony opened the door to the Bronco, slid behind the wheel, and backed around to get on the road, he asked, "O.K., what all's goin' on around here, anyway?"

Misty brought him up on all the happenings of the day—the trip to Lawford's, the majestic Arabian, the damaged telephone, the uneasy ride home and her father's concern about the missing cattle.

Tony said in disbelief, "Humvee's? Why would army Humvee's be around here?" Then after a while he added, "I can't wait to see that horse. Must really be something."

"Believe me, he is something," said Misty softly.

"I can see why the sheriff won't come to look after the missing cattle, though," Tony said. "What's to do? If the McAndrews' can't find those calves, how could the Sheriff? I can't see, though, why he won't file a report. I'm sure the ranchers have papers to prove they existed."

"Well, I guess it's kind of like a missing person— most of the time, they've just run away 'cause they don't like where they were, and they turn up in a few days. I'd bet, though, if the sheriff *doesn't* come out, and if the calves *don't* turn up, those ranchers will do somethin', and Sheriff Calahan better find a new job come fall elections," said Misty.

"Umm, hmm," Tony agreed.

He'd heard his father say many times that he "never heard of a crook bein' caught with a horseshoe" or "I just can't see what bein' horseshoe champion has to do with keepin' the peace. All the good sheriff does is practice his horseshoe game behind the post office in Littleville."

But Tony wasn't sure the sheriff was so bad. "Well, the sheriff's got a lot of things to think about." Tony paused, thinking. "He headed up those two raids on the meth factories last month that put away both the Sandler boys."

"Yeah, but most people felt that shoulda happened a long time ago. Everyone knew they had to be doin' somethin' in that locked potato cellar," argued Misty, "and the sheriff didn't do that alone. The federal guys were the ones who actually made the raid."

"Yeh. but he laid all the groundwork," said Tony, "and besides, it had to take a lot of nerve to arrest the sons of the newspaper editor. D'she leave town yet?"

"Nope, she's still livin' out there, takin' care a those pigs," Misty answered.

Melissa Sandler was the editor of *The Littleville Gazette*, the closest town's weekly newspaper. Between editions, she raised pot-bellied pigs and three closemouthed, unruly boys in a run-down brick building that had been a rural grade school before the county's schools had consolidated into Goldenrod. Her husband had left some years ago—about eight years ago—since that was the age of Cicero, her youngest—a round, quiet boy with rosy cheeks and solemn gray eyes.

Brett and Brady were the oldest. Sixteen and seventeen years old, they had both been in the same graduating class the previous spring. No one seemed to know why they were in the same grade, or why they were so young for their class; most of the other students were at least 18 when they received their diplomas. In their senior year at school, they had been the most notorious truants in the county—never disappearing until after first period when role was taken, but then sulking into their classes at random. Their mother always gave them a post-absentee excuse, however, and even with their spotty attendance records, they had both graduated with respectable standings. They had even made high scores on their college entrance exams—and because of their good scores and their mother's low income, were offered scholarships to several state colleges. They just never got around to enrolling at any of them.

From the time her boys were arraigned, Mrs. Sandler had filled the editorial page, writing about the unjustness of her boys' arrest and saying she would close the newspaper and leave town if the boys were convicted—throwing accusations and insults at the town, the sheriff and the county judge. The editorials were so entertaining that she didn't lose any of her readers or advertisers. In fact, subscriptions and the number of ads increased, for despite her squalid domestic situation, her failures as a disciplinarian, and her neglect of her skinny, formless body, Melissa Sandler was an able newspaperwoman and a colorful writer. She had won several awards for her well-edited weekly, and her articles were often published in the Omaha World Herald and other newspapers around the state.

Some of this recognition was at the expense of her only brother, Kevin Belle. He and Melissa had been feuding for years. Melissa called Kevin a "capitalist pig" because he ran a big ranch operation that belonged to outsiders. Melissa believed that no matter what, ranches should be owned and operated by the local families who live on them.

Controversy, Melissa style, drew everyone's attention, whether they agreed with her or not. There had not been an issue of the *Gazette* since the boys were found guilty, and most everyone in five counties missed the paper.

In a few minutes Tony and Misty were home, and when they drove into the yard, they were surprised to find an unfamiliar car parked beside their mother's Range Rover and their father's SUV. It was a long, black luxury sedan. Closer inspection revealed leather seats and Colorado plates.

"That's weird," said Misty. "Wonder where that car came from. Nothin' passed by while we were loadin' the calf."

"Musta come up the hill road from Lawfords," guessed Tony. "There's a lot of washouts on that road, though. That'd be quite a ride in that Mafiamobile."

They parked their vehicles near the back sheds. Tony and Misty jumped from the Bronco and joined Hank as he came around the front of his truck.

"Whose car is that?" asked Tony.

"Not sure," said his father. "From the license plate, I'd guess it's a rental car—probably somebody flew into Denver then drove here—."

"But nobody came past us—," interrupted Misty.

"Musta come from Lawford's the back way," Hank mused.

"One of mom's friends?" asked Misty doubtfully.

"Hardly," said her father. "More likely Scooter Lawford. When I tried to find John this afternoon, I called Scooter's office in California, and they said he was away for the weekend—goin' to the midwest to see his father. Maybe that's where John's been—meetin' Scooter at the airport."

In the house, they removed their coats at the back door, kicked off their boots and then turned softly down the hall to the living room.

"Well, I'm sure John's just fine—probably just gone off to a horse sale somewhere," Angela West was saying. She was standing in front of the fireplace holding a cup and saucer, still wearing her sweat-suit and trainers. Ben was slumped into the corner of his father's favorite oversized rocker. Scooter Lawford was sitting on the hassock in front of the sofa.

John Lawford's tall son had aged in the two years or so since the West family had last seen him; his hair was grayer and molded into a sparse, lacquered crew cut. His face was softer and rounder with a chin that tugged at the corners of his mouth and puffed into his neck. Small rimless glasses sat partway down his straight nose. He rose as Hank padded over in his stocking feet to shake his hand. "Thought that big, city-slicker, Dick-Tracy car might be yours," Hank grinned.

"It was about the only thing left at the airport that I thought might make it on these roads," Scooter replied as he grasped Hank's hand. "All the SUV's and off-road types were taken; something going on up in the mountains, and there's an ice storm and high winds up there."

"Probably be rain down here tomorrow then," sighed Hank. "Well, I'm glad you're here. I take it from what I heard comin' in that you don't know where your father is either. Angela probably told you I called all over this afternoon tryin' ta—ta find him." Hank sneezed loudly, took a handkerchief from his back pocket and blew his nose. "Damned allergies."

"Yeah, that's what she said. I realize Dad's become pretty independent since Ma died and George left, but isn't it pretty unusual for him to go away without telling you—or telling anyone else in town?"

Everyone in the room but Scooter nodded or kept expressionless faces of agreement, and he went on. "I talked to Brenda at Jigs. She hasn't seen him since Friday." Jigs was the only restaurant in Littleville—located on the second floor of a hotel that had been open since the late 1800's. John ate breakfast there most mornings when he came in to get his mail from a post office box he rented.

"Yup, that's what she told me, too," agreed Hank.

"I told him last month I was coming, but when I called yesterday and this afternoon to let him know what time I'd be here, the phone was dead again. I left two e-mail messages, but didn't get a reply before I left. The phone was working fine when I got there this afternoon. I wish he'd get a cell phone. I left a message for him to call here if he came home." Scooter turned sideways, so he could see all of them, including Ben. "When was the last time any of you saw him?"

"I haven't seen John since I had breakfast with him and Putty Rand just after Labor Day," said Hank.

"I don't think I've seen him since Tony and me went fishin' over at Alkalai Lake a couple a weeks ago," said Ben. "He was with some other fella. They were parked on the other side of the lake, and John came over to borrow some minnows. Said the other fella was some guy he went to college with. Never did meet him though."

Tony agreed. "Yeah, I think that's the last time I saw him, too."

"Well, I've seen him since then," said Angela thoughtfully. "He passed me up in his green pickup when I was driving into Kilpatrick last Saturday."

"He *passed* you?" Tony's eyes widened in mock surprise. Angela had been given two speeding tickets in the past month. "Ya mean *you* let somebody go around you?"

"Hush, you!" his mother scowled, embarrassed. "Yes, and he was driving at a pretty good clip. I remember being surprised at how fast he was going. That isn't like John. He's a pretty careful driver. I didn't see that anyone was with him, though."

There was a pause before Misty finally said, "I might have seen him, but I'm not sure. I *thought* I saw his pickup parked outside Sandler's place when I went to orchestra practice Monday afternoon. I can't say for sure it was John's, but it was a pickup just like his, and it had a couple of bails of hay in the back—like he takes out to feed his horses sometimes."

"Why would John be visiting Mrs. Sandler?" asked Tony doubtfully.

Misty shrugged. "Why not?" She paused. "Maybe she's havin' a moving sale."

"Hope springs eternal," sighed Angela. "Maybe somebody will buy that place and clean up all the junk in the yard."

Scooter stood. "Well, I think it's time to call Sheriff Calahan," he said. "Could be something's not right. Dad may just be out looking at horses—or visiting a friend, but I'll feel better when I know where he is."

Hank motioned toward the door. "Come on back t'my office and we'll give Al Calahan a call—ask 'im t'come out here. I've got a couple of other things I'd like to talk to him about." They started out of the room, then Hank turned back. "Misty, you come with us and fill Scooter in on what you saw this afternoon," then, "Hon, can you set another place at the table?"

"Sure thing," she answered, and with a scowl, she looked back at the boys. "You boys get cleaned up a bit. We're having a guest for dinner."

The boys started up the stairs, and Angela followed, "I'm going to get in the shower too. I smell like a truck driver."

Chapter Six

They were six around the table; Claire had left only five pot pies, so Angela and Misty had to share one, which wasn't a hardship, since each puffy, golden pie was about the size of half a bowling ball. Claire Cooper had grown up in a family of ten and had never learned to cook anything in moderate portions. Most of her specialties included a flaky pastry crust or a heavy, peppery covering of gravy, but she also made exotic green salads and vegetables that were flavored with the herbs she grew in the makeshift hothouse behind the old chickenless chicken coop. Tonight there was also a salad of arugula, chick peas and red onions in a spicy dressing. A pan of lemon bars were sliced for dessert.

Ben rang the hallway dinner bell after the boys had helped Angela get the food on the table. As they all met in the dining room and prepared to settle into the tall, ladder-back chairs that circled the big oak table, Angela asked, "So, did you get Sheriff Calahan?"

"Yeah, we got hold of him," Hank answered. "He was pretty shook up about John, took information and sent out bulletins while we were on the line. Think he might be rememberin' that old fella that wandered off last year, and they found him dead in a ditch six months later." He looked up at Scooter across the table. "Sorry, Scooter, I don't mean to make you think that might have happened to your dad." Then he added, "They're goin' to send out the 'copter first thing tomorrow morning if John hasn't turned up. I told 'em we could take Hooter out too if they wanted."

He took a piece of brown bread from a plate that was being passed in front of him. "Said he'd come out tomorrow t'look at the Dutch Belted steer." He looked at his wife. "The kids and I brought home a dead steer that I'm pretty sure belongs to Jimmy McAndrews—found it just north of Stoop's Corner."

Angela scowled.

Hank went on, "The sheriff didn't seem to give a damn about Jimmy's other cattle though, said he'd file a report one of these days if they didn't turn up. I called Jim; he's fit to be tied. He's comin' over in the morning too."

"That's a shame about the calf." Angela paused, then added, "One of us can certainly fly part of the search pattern if it comes to that." She turned to Scooter. "Do you think that's really necessary at this point?"

"I don't know, but if he isn't home by morning, I'd feel better if we checked out the ranch, especially with those Hummers and all." Scooter built a big haystack of salad on his plate.

"Hummers?" Angela scowled as she ground pepper onto her pot pie.

"Ben and I saw two Humvees in the hills when we were watching the Arabians today," Misty put in quickly. "Didn't know any of the drivers, at least not that we could tell through the glasses."

"Isn't that an unusual vehicle to see in this part of the country?"

51

"That's pretty much what we thought, Angela," said Scooter, "But I didn't see them, nor did I see anything else out of line when I was at the house. I drove out to Apple Rock, then came over here to see what you folks knew. Everything seemed fine along the way, but if dad doesn't come home by morning, we'd like to cover as much territory as we can by air—to see what we see from up there." He poked a hole in the top of his pie and smiled as he inhaled the fragrant steam that curled out. "Honestly, though, I'd bet the old man'll come bumpin' home in the middle of the night—probably up to Casper or Rapid City or somewhere—looking for more Arabians. And those guys on those machines were just joy riders."

And who cut the cord on our bag phone? Misty thought, but, as her father had pointed out, they weren't sure the cord was intact when Misty and Ben left for Lawford's. Thinking about the frightened horses, she said, "If there is a fly-over, we have to be careful to make sure we don't scare the horses." She looked at Ben. "Scooter says he didn't know anything about the new Arabian—didn't even know his dad had a new horse."

"Yeah, I gave him a digital camera for Christmas a couple of years ago. He usually sends me an e-mail with a picture every time he gets a new pony to add to the herd. The last I got was of a reddish bay broodmare out of some farm in Kentucky. That was about three months ago. Haven't had one since."

"Well, I woulda thought he'd for sure sent you a picture of this one. He's gotta be proud of him," said

Ben before he took a big bite of the thick bread he had covered with butter and cherry jam.

"This horse is like no horse I've ever seen," agreed Misty. "We named him Mirage, because he's kind of too good to be true. He carries himself like royalty or something. And he's so big. I've never seen an Arabian this size."

"How big is he," asked Scooter.

"I'd say almost 16 hands," said Ben.

"That could be a problem," said Scooter. "Most Arabians who are over 15 hands get their height from long legs and straight shoulders—and those legs are most times too spindly to support them properly." Scooter grinned. "Kind of like that chair in the corner that Angela won't let us men sit on, because she's afraid we'll break it. It's better to have an Arabian like these oak chairs, with shorter, stronger legs. Short, strong bones, well-developed muscles, and good joints make a fast horse."

"Well, it looked to me like this horse has good legs, and he has powerful shoulders," said Misty. "He's wonderfully well-proportioned—and strong, and when he runs, it's like he's floating. You should see how his neck arches, and how he holds his head up. I mean all of your dad's horses are beautiful, but this one gives you goosebumps."

"I love watching the Arabians," said Tony. "It seems to me most of 'em do keep their heads up high when they run. Maybe it's 'cause they know they're blue-bloods and they wanta show off their high cheekbones." He looked at Scooter. "I remember reading though, that the way they hold their heads and arch their throats—and the way their cheekbones are spaced wide apart like they are—make room for an extra large windpipe. Makes it easier for them to breathe a lot of air, both in and out. In fact, once I heard Mr. Lawford call them 'drinkers of the wind'— said that it came from an old Arab legend."

"Uh-huh, did he tell you the legend?" asked Scooter.

"No, I was just sort of eavesdropping," said Tony.

Scooter nodded. "The story is that God—or Allah—had a great love for the south wind and wanted to give it life, so he created Arabian horses by folding the wind into itself. That way the wind would always be at the horses' center." He looked up at Tony. "And that's true in a way, because just as you said, an enlarged windpipe allows them to bring in more air, so they retain more oxygen. That gives them more stamina than almost any other breed of horse."

"Your dad told me once that the Arabians were the reason the Christian knights lost to the Muslims in the crusades of the middle ages," said Misty. "Those big, clumsy horses the Europeans were using to carry all that armor were just no match for them. The Arabian horses were just so much faster and smarter and never seemed to get tired."

"How'd your dad get interested in Arabians, anyway?" asked Tony.

Scooter glanced at Hank. "Whoa, that's a long story," he said, "I'm surprised my dad or your dad didn't ever tell you about it."

"Well?" said Tony, expectantly.

"Let's save it for after dinner," Angela cut in. "First, I'd like to hear about the contest you almost won today."

"'Almost won' in any language means *lost*," Tony said irritably, then after a moment, he shrugged and smiled. Everything that had happened since he turned off at Stoops corner had distracted him and softened his disappointment at not winning the contest. Never one to neglect a fresh audience, he set about translating their loss through a cluster of ironic and amusing stories that only Tony could have wrung out of a contest in mathematics. Misty and Ben laughed enthusiastically in relief.

Chapter Seven

After dinner, they tried once again to reach Mr. Lawford by telephoning his home. There was no answer, nor were there any messages when Scooter checked in with his message service in California. He also used a remote access code to check the message machine at his father's house. There was nothing there either.

That done, everyone settled in the living room with two pots of herbal tea and the lemon bars. Scooter sought out Angela's favorite piece of furniture, a kangaroo sofa with a gradually sloping back and a graceful, looping Rococo frame. He draped himself onto the tufted red velvet that had faded to a watery raspberry, poured himself a cup of tea, stared into the fire and began to talk about his father and the Arabians.

"Well, I guess it makes more sense to start at the beginning. As you all probably know, the Arabians were the horses of the deserts in the Arab countries. My dad says they've been known as a distinct breed of horses for over 3,500 years. You might have seen pictures of ancient hieroglyphics that show horses that look exactly like today's Arabians pulling the Pharaohs' chariots. Some of those sketches were drawn in about 1500 BC. As a doctor, I can tell you it makes sense that Arabians would do well in those hot climates, because their circulatory systems have arteries and veins that're close to the surface. That, combined with their thin skins helps them to cool off faster than other horses. Their dark hides keep the horses from getting burned in the hot sun—and the way they carry their tails in the air helps keep them cool too."

Scooter cleared his throat. "Not only do Arabians do well in the heat, they have incredible endurance and strength—and they're loyal—and they have courage. There's a legend that says that either the Prophet Mohammed—or a horseman known as Faris—both men have been credited as the hero in this story—decided to test his Arabians to see how brave and devoted they were. He took 100 of his best mares and put them in a pen and gave them no water for about a week. When he finally let them out, the thirsty mares started out for a creek to get a drink of water. Their leader blew the horn then—a call to battle—and five of the mares turned and came back to him. These were the five chosen as mothers for the breed. I don't know if this story is true or not, but I do know that Misty was right, history has proven them to be the greatest war-horses that ever were."

Scooter blew on the hot tea in his cup, took a sip, and then went on. "My ma knew everything about Arabians. She categorized them as the Kuhaylan, a strong, more masculine horse, and the Saklawi, the finer boned, more feminine lineage. It's interesting that as they were imported into other countries, they developed like the tale of the mares—into five main bloodlines: English, Russian, Polish, Spanish, and Egyptian, and each of these countries bred the Arabians to different strengths. For instance, the Russians wanted Arabians with stamina and endurance. They had Arabians that could perform even in the harshest conditions. That line is stronger and generally more resistant to disease."

He stared into his cup, then looked up and went on. "Then there's Poland. Poland has been famous for breeding powerful, agile, and beautiful Arabian horses for a long time—for hundreds of years. The Poles were more interested in racing. Bred their Arabians to make them as fast as possible.

The English have some fast horses too, thanks to the Arabians. In the late 1600's and early 1700's— after the crusades—Arabian horses were imported into England and interbred with the heavier English horses. Out came some of the fastest horses alive. Since then, they've mixed all sorts of breeds with Arabians. As I'm sure you know, all Thoroughbred racehorses— maybe even all light horses—are descendants of Arabians." He smiled at Misty.

"The first Arabian my dad could track down that came over here was a stallion that some guy by the name of Harrison brought to America in the early 1700's. His Arabian fathered about 300 offspring. George Washington rode one of his descendants during the Revolutionary War."

Scooter stretched his legs out in front of him, ran his hand over the top of his crew cut, took a deep swallow of the tea, and set the cup on the floor.

"My ma actually started it all in our family. The Arabian bug bit her when she was working horses on a stud farm around Estes Park, Colorado, in the early 1960's. The ranchers on the place next to where she was working raised Arabians and had leased a bay stallion called Aksamit for stud. She just fell head over heels for that horse. After she'd exercised the horses that belonged to the people she worked for, she'd stop by and watch that big Arabian.

By all accounts I guess this was one beautiful stallion—a stunning example of the Kuhaylan, the more athletic and heavier strain of Arabians. We have a picture of Aksamit on the bookshelves in our house. My ma put it there. You might have seen it; it shows this great bay with a big star on his forehead, a snip on his nose, and matching white stockings on all four feet. Anyway, even though he was about 25 years old when my ma first saw him, she fell in love with him. I think part of it might have been his romantic past. There was so much intrigue in Aksamit's life that I think a couple of books and a movie script have even been written about him."

"Why? What happened to him?" Misty asked as she raised up from where she was lying in front of the fire. After seeing the Arabian she now called Mirage, Misty could understand how you could fall for a horse—love at first sight.

"Well," Scooter went on, "seems Aksamit was born on a stud farm in Poland some time in 1938. During World War II, when the Germans invaded Poland—some time in 1939, Aksamit was just about a year old. The owners of the horses on the farm tried to disguise him by smearing him with mud to make him look like a workhorse so the Germans wouldn't want him, but it didn't work. The Germans found him anyway. They took good care of him though, bringing in German veterinarians and horse experts to make sure that he and all the other fancy horses they found on that stud farm were well cared for. Then, when the war was almost over, the Germans who were taking care of the horses got scared. They were losing the war, and they were afraid the horses would be taken—or eaten—by the hungry Russian army that was just over the hill. I guess they thought the U.S. was the lesser of two evils. They made a plea to the U.S. Army to get the horses out before the Russians came—and one of the U.S. commanders agreed to help.

This commander—George Patton—was a cavalry officer and a superb horseman. He knew that many of Europe's Arabians were already lost or dead, and he wanted to save the few that were left. A couple of the German veterinarians risked their lives to sneak across between the trenches during the night and meet with the Americans to set up a plan to make sure all of the horses were evacuated. More than 250 beautiful horses were moved. I remember my dad told me there were Lipizzans, Thoroughbreds, Andulusians, Clydesdales and some other breeds as well—along with the Arabians. The soldiers either rode them or shipped them through Czechoslovakia into Austria in big army trucks with open beds; they had to go over 200 miles of very bad roads. Later they put the best of the Arabians on a boat and shipped them to the states. That's how Aksamit got over here."

Scooter paused to refill his cup, then sat on the edge of the sofa.

"Anyway, after my ma got interested in that horse, she did some research and discovered that his papa was one of the greatest stallions in Poland. That didn't surprise her, but it was what she found out about Aksamit's mama that really got her hooked. The mare's name was Ksiezna—K-s-i-e-z-n-a—I'm probably not pronouncing it right. I think it means princess in Polish. At any rate, her color was a run-of-the mill gray, but she had something special—a patch of red-brown across her withers. The people of the Bedouin desert called it a "bloody shoulder" and thought it to be a "mark of Allah." They believed that any horse with that marking was mystic, that the horse would be exceptional and would produce wondrous offspring. Well, Aksamit was indeed a hero of a horse. He won lots of ribbons and sired a stunning string of champions. My ma used to keep a scrapbook of 'em." Scooter looked up at Hank, who nodded that he remembered.

"Sometime in 1964, Aksamit left the place next to where my ma was working, and at about the same time, my ma met my dad. They were married and moved out here and took over the ranch, so Grandma and Grandpa Lawford could move to their place in Arizona. No more than six months after Ma and Dad moved to the ranch, my ma had her first Arabian, a gray stallion who had contracted some kind of virus while he was on the ship coming from Egypt to the U.S. A high fever had made him sterile. Since he couldn't stand to stud, and his owners thought his skittish temperament made him no good as a show horse, he was considered worthless as an investment. Ma bought him for less than $500."

Ben whistled softly.

Scooter nodded. "His name was Horus—the name of one of the ancient Egyptian gods of sunlight, my ma said. I think he was of the Saklawi, the more fine-boned lineage of Arabians. He had kind of a narrow chest and a long face with a tapered nose, large, flared nostrils and very sunken cheeks. He grew whiter as he became older. His eyes were set wide apart, and they were immense—and dark—and deep. He was very arresting.

As a small child, I remember standing on the fence when he was in summer pasture, feeding him sugar cubes, wondering what made him look so sad. Ma said the sad look came from how he'd been treated in Egypt, because where he'd been raised, stallions were kept in their stalls almost all the time and were only fed a certain kind of hay and maybe some dates. They were never allowed to run free. She would actually get tears in her eyes when she thought of this beautiful, spirited animal confined to a space no bigger than her kitchen pantry.

My dad was the one who started to ride him—the one who really calmed him down. He said he thought the horse's bad temperament had come from being confined in such a small space for so long. Horus had so much energy. I remember my dad flying down the back hill road riding bareback on that white horse. After he trained him to western saddle, Ma started riding him. She took him to horse shows all over Nebraska, Colorado, and Wyoming. She dressed him in a showy saddle and bridle, and she wore a sparkly Arabic costume made out of gauzy stuff that drifted in the breeze—and believe it or not—even a veil of the same stuff. She and Horus were always a big hit. I rode him too when I was older. He was the smartest horse I ever got on top of.

Horus was the first, and Ma never stopped looking. My dad was good at ranching, and he made the place pay off a lot better than my grandfather had. Good thing too. They spent a lot of money; we used to go to Houston, Los Angeles, Denver, Nashville, lots of places in Canada—anywhere there was a horse show that included Arabians. Ma and Dad knew everyone in the U. S. of A. who had Arabian horses, and they bought more. I especially remember a couple that really set my dad back a pretty penny: two mares, one named Al-Naher Diane and another named Satyna June. A good share of the ribbons and trophies that are hangin' in my dad's office were earned by their offspring." Scooter paused. "But they couldn't find the horse my ma wanted. She had her heart set on a stallion from the line of Ksiezna with the bloody shoulder."

Scooter stared into the fire.

"I guess I was about 15 when I answered the phone one morning before I left for school, and a man with a heavy accent asked to speak to my father. They talked for quite a while; they were still talking when I left for school. When I came home that night, Ma and Dad were sitting at the kitchen table. They were both lookin' pretty grim, but there was a kind of excitement in the air as well.

'Scooter,' he said when I asked was going on, 'We may have a chance to get one of the Arabians we want.

The only problem is that I may have to go into Communist Poland to get it.'

Well, in 1979, Poland was part of the Communist Bloc and to us here in the states, it was a forbidden and heavily guarded no-mans-land. The man who had called my father was from West Germany, and he knew a man in Poland who wanted to make a trade. He had a son who wanted to leave the country to go to school in the United States—and he had a stallion he said was the grandson of Ksiezna with the bloody shoulder. Somehow he had learned that my father and mother were looking for such a horse, and he wanted to trade that horse for his son's escape."

"How did your father know the man from Poland wasn't lying about his horse's lineage?" Tony asked.

Scooter nodded at Tony. "Good Question. My dad said the man in Poland had sent a copy of the horse's studbook records to the man in Germany, and he had had them authenticated, so my folks were convinced this man had one of the horses they wanted."

"Why did the man's son want to come to the U.S.?" asked Misty.

"He was a young writer—a very good one by all accounts—and what he wanted to write, the communist government wouldn't let him publish. In fact, his parents were pretty worried that the thought police were already after him." Scooter sat upright and set his teacup on the round table in front of the sofa. He wiped his face with his hands. "The plan was that the Pole and another man from the stud farm were going to put the son into a false bottom in one of the state-owned horse trailers. They had bribed some guards at the border, saying they were going to do some horse trading, going to bring in a couple of horses that would improve the breed of Thoroughbreds in the stables at the state stud farms. And that was truly what they were doing—the stud farm needed new Thoroughbred breeding stallions.

Well, horses and racing are big deal now in Poland, but they were even more so during the cold war, when there wasn't a lot to feel good about in most Poles' daily lives. The guards saw themselves as purveyors of improvements in horse racing, and they agreed to take the man's bribe, which, by the way, was made up of his entire life savings and some of his parents' jewelry he'd managed to keep hidden."

Scooter cleared his throat. "So the plan was that my dad was going to fly to West Germany and purchase two Thoroughbreds and a two-horse trailer—which had been painted to look like those on the stud farm—from the man who had made contact with him. The man's name was Herr Wolfmann, and my dad paid him a lot of money for the horses and the trailer, probably much more than they were worth.

He and Herr Wolfmann left West Germany about midnight armed with papers—some false, and some legitimate—and drove through East Germany. That was a very dangerous trip in those times. East German soldiers had very itchy trigger fingers, and my dad and the German were at the mercy of the East German police and government officials if they got into any kind of pickle.

They were driving an old pickup, pulling the trailer toward a border crossing at a place called Sczezin. The plan was that once there they would trade their trailer for the one the Pole brought with him. The trailers looked just the same, but their trailer had two horses, and the one coming out of Poland had only one horse inside—and the Polish man's son, of course. The trip there and back was about 300 miles."

"How old was the son?" Ben asked.

"I think he was about 17," Scooter replied. "I guess he wasn't very big, and his father had built a shallow compartment over the floor of the trailer. My dad said it was hard to tell it was even there. There were air holes at the top, but there was no door; the boy was nailed in."

Misty, Ben, and Tony raised their heads and frowned in disbelief.

"Anyway—," said Scooter. His voice had grown softer and his tone more serious. "When they got to the border, sure enough, the trailer was waiting, and the Pole insisted that my father inspect the Arabian he had brought to trade. Dad said he pretended to inspect the horse, but he had no memory of it, because he was trying so hard not to look for the compartment in the trailer where the man's son was hiding. Then they all had to have a drink of some kind of Polish liquor with the guards. Of course, my father said nothing but 'Ja' and 'Nein,' afraid that what little German he knew would betray his American accent. Finally the guards let them hook up the other trailer, and they started on their way.

About half-way to the West German border, it started to rain, and the East German roads—like almost everything else in East Germany at that time—were in terrible condition. Twice, they slid off the road when they were trying to avoid potholes, and once one of the wheels on the trailer got buried in the mud. Dad said they would never have got the trailer out if a local farmer and his son hadn't come out to help them. At any rate, instead of a three-hour trip back to West Germany, they were on the road for over 12 hours.

I guess there were additional holdups at the border getting back into West Germany, but they finally crossed the border and drove to a safe place where they could release the young man. They led the Arabian out of the horse trailer and set about removing the nails from the end of the compartment. As they began to do that, they became sick. Between the weight of the horse, the poor quality of the nails and wood the Poles had to use, and the moisture that had come in the sides of the trailer to soak and soften the wood, the false floor had sunk about two inches. When they finally got to the young man, he was dead; he had suffocated when part of the floor had crushed his chest."

None of those in the room moved. No one even breathed for a moment. All of them, including Scooter, had tears in their eyes.

"My dad decided right then and there that he would never be party to the imprisonment of anything ever again—that any person or animal under his care would be as free as he could arrange for them to be." Scooter rubbed at his eyes with his fingers. "That horse's name was Mrok; we called him Shadow—a beautiful gray. He's out there somewhere."

The only sound was the heavy tick-tock of the grandfather clock until Scooter added, "And the ironic thing is—that after all that—that horse has never given us a foal with a bloody shoulder."

Chapter Eight

"Rise and shine, beauty bee!" Hank walked over to the east window and opened the shade to expose the orange light from the first morning sky. He was dressed in riding denims and a sheep-lined leather mackinaw. "Come on Misty, the sun's up, and we wanta get started as soon as we can."

"So Mr. Lawford didn't come home?" Misty sat up and ran her hand back through her hair to get it out of her face.

"Nope, and Scooter's gettin' worried. The sheriff's gonna meet us at Lawfords with the 'copter. Your mom and Ben already left with Hooter. Tony's on his way over to Nolde's; he and Lono and her dad are gonna take out the ATV's and scour the south end."

That made sense. Nolde's had recently acquired some property that bordered both the Lawford's and the West's for just a couple of miles on the south edge of both ranches, and the long bluffs down there were covered with trees. The all-terrain vehicles would be perfect for searching that area, because you couldn't see much from the air.

"What're *we* gonna do?" Misty asked as she pulled back the covers and sat on the edge of the bed.

"You and I are gonna ride with Scooter—get a good look at those horses, see if there are any more new ones—see if he can tell if any are missin'—or if anything else isn't quite right." Hank paused at the door. "You better put on your long handles. There's a

69

good winter bluster out there—even a few snow flakes."

"What about Jimmy McAndrews?" Misty asked as she doubled her flannel nightgown around her, anticipating the bite of the early morning cold.

"Talked to him a few minutes ago. We're gonna bring the sheriff back here later. Jimmy's comin' over then. It's not supposed to get much above freezing today, so that calf should keep. Meantime, Jimmy's gonna do some checkin' by phone—see if John's at any of his old haunts Jimmy knows about in Omaha." Hank turned to go down the hall. "Better get a move on, so they won't be waitin' on us."

Ten minutes later, Misty was in the kitchen mixing a thermos of hot chocolate. She was dressed in a turtleneck and jeans on the outside, a layer of thermal underwear on the inside. Her heavy down coat and a ski mask lay on the bench beside the back door. She picked a bag of frozen muffins from the freezer and stuffed them into the lunch box beside the thermos.

Her father came stomping in with his buckskin boots. "I have our horses saddled and in the trailer. Let's go."

They were at Lawford's ranch in half an hour. Scooter rode up to meet them. He sat comfortably on his father's working horse, a stout pinto, and watched Misty and her father unload their horses from the trailer. Misty led Cadaver, the family horse that everyone on the ranch rode from time to time. Her father had his favorite, a strong, Irish draft gelding named Sumo. The horse had a big, egg-shaped head and powerful muscles in his thighs. He was a tireless dark tan bay, even-tempered most of the time, but he had tendency to nip at strangers—animal or human. As Sumo came down the ramp, he eyed John Lawford's two shaggy and freckled blue heelers. They were circling the pinto with their tails wagging, hoping for a long run.

When all three were mounted, they rode outside the gate to where the helicopter was sitting. Sheriff Calahan and his deputy, Will Krause, were leaning against the cab and nodded a welcome. Hooter, gliding overhead, made a wide turn, then Angela tipped its wings in greeting.

"I guess we'll follow the plan we talked about earlier. Angela's got her map. I charted it out, so between us, we have the open areas pretty much covered." The sheriff reached under his sheepskin-lined denim jacket to jerk up the belt at the front of his jeans. He was a big man in early middle age with heavy brown hair and gray eyes that stared hard to subdue others and blinked whenever he was nervous. His voice had a raspy edge, and, as always, he wore steel-tipped alligator-skin cowboy boots. They were black today.

Deputy Will was the pilot. He was tall with longish dull black hair, lazy eyes, and warm green coveralls. He was a former Army Ranger and part-time lawman who made the payments on his double-wide by blowing insulation made from gray newsprint into the empty walls and attics of the old farm and ranch houses that were perched on the prairie. He used a noisy machine that he carried around in a purple van that had "Indoor Weather Control" painted with neon green lettering on both sides.

"Well, we're gonna just generally check around—look for the horses—and follow up on anything else we see that doesn't seem in line," said Misty's father. "We'll meet you back here around noon."

"Sounds good," said the sheriff.

The three riders turned back to the ranch and followed the same path Misty and Ben had taken the day before—across a series of rolling hills to a short cut that led to Apple Rock. Once there, they studied the horses' tracks from the day before. A relentless October wind still dragged through the pass, obscuring the hoof marks in the fine prairie sand. There were no fresh tracks, so it looked as though the herd had not been back this way. The three riders turned to head north, in the direction the horses had taken when Misty and Ben had seen them last. After they had ridden about half an hour, they heard Hooter's motor buzzing overhead. As it came near, the plane dipped, and they could see Ben motioning to the right.

As one, they turned their horses in that direction.

Misty saw them first—as their mounts were trudging to the top of a long hill. The two men had their heads down against the wind, but Misty was looking over to the east. She spotted some of the herd huddled and resting about two miles off, in the shelter of a blowout where the prairie gales had carved a cave of protection in the side of a hill. The wind was out of the northeast, and the sand was soft on the hills, so the horses hadn't sensed their approach. She pulled up, and the men did likewise.

"Do you have the glasses?" Misty's father asked her after she had pointed out the horses.

She handed the binoculars to him without comment, and after he had removed the lense covers, he raised them to his eyes.

"Well, I see the gray. He's at the back by those junipers." Hank handed the glasses to Scooter.

Scooter walked the pinto to the right about 10 yards, stopped, and sighted the horses through the powerful glasses. "Yea, that's what I thought. That gray is Shadow, the horse my dad brought back from Poland. Looks like he's favoring the front right leg. Well, he's no youngster—must be goin' on 23 or 24."

"He's still a beautiful horse," said Misty. "But he was movin' funny when we saw him yesterday too. Ben and I thought maybe the new stallion had challenged him for the lead and he got hurt. Do you see him? Mirage, I mean?"

"Hard to say," Scooter said tentatively as he peered through the binoculars. "Some of the horses are lying down; some are standing in front of others, and there's a windmill and a horse tank to the right that obscure the rest. I can't say I see any that would fit the description you gave me last night."

Finally he handed the glasses back to Hank and said, "Tell you what. As you know, this is my dad's horse I'm on, and I'm wearin' his sheepskin." He looked down at the dogs sitting in the grass, panting from the long run. "The horses are used to these dogs, and he rides this pinto whenever he goes out to check on the herd. Why don't I go down first? You two stay back 20 yards or so. Maybe we can get close to 'em this way."

Hank and Misty nodded, and Scooter started down the hill. He rode carefully, walking the horse through the wind-driven buffalo grass, moving slowly and deliberately toward the herd. When he was about 100 yards to the south of the first cluster of horses, the animals raised their heads and studied the rider on the spotted horse. A few of them turned to look to the inside of the hill. Within a few seconds, a dark shadow emerged from behind a sandy swell on which a single tree grew sideways, its branches flapping in the wind like the arms of a stringless puppet. Behind the displaced tree, a dusky silhouette seemed to gather a dark velvet body about it, and when it stepped out, it was the splendid Arabian that Misty called Mirage standing in the cold light at the edge of the herd. The wind whistled around the trees and fought its way across the prairie, making primitive sounds that added an eerie mysticism to the horse's presence.

Using the glasses, Misty could see he was at least a hand higher than most of the other horses, a true liver chestnut, chocolate brown with one white pastern above the hoof on his left foreleg. He stood with his front legs wide apart, and his small ears were up. He seemed cautious, but he didn't show that he was afraid or threatened.

Scooter signaled for the dogs to stay where they were and pressured the pinto gently with his knees to urge the horse slowly forward. The others in the herd watched the man on the pinto intently, but didn't move. When he was about 20 feet from the big

Arabian, Scooter slid slowly out of his saddle and began to walk toward the horse, and then he stood still, watching the stallion. Surprisingly, the big Arabian came forward—toward Scooter. Scooter very cautiously extracted some sugar cubes his father had left in the pocket of his jacket and extended them on his palm. The horse hesitated—then come forward to sniff his hand. When he had eaten all the sugar, he looked at Scooter expectantly, then stepped up to put his nose to the pocket from which the treats had been taken. Some of the other horses edged forward then, but stopped 10 yards or so from where Scooter stood with the regal stallion.

He offered more cubes of sugar, and as the horse nibbled at them, he raised his hand to pet the animal's elegant neck. His hand stopped in mid-air. He hadn't noticed from a distance, but there it was—the bloody shoulder, the mark of Allah—a patch that was more red than brown amidst the dark of the stallion's coat. Scooter stood for many minutes, staring at the horse's withers as he offered the treats and stroked the stallion's shoulder and back. When the horse was satisfied the pocket was empty, he pulled away from Scooter's hand and trotted back to the herd. The other horses followed, and soon they all moved out behind the horse Misty called Mirage, staying close to the shelter of the hills in the distance.

The faithful pinto moved up to bump Scooter's shoulder as they watched the herd's ragged retreat, but Scooter remained, still and silent, seemingly untouched by the frigid wind and patchy sleet that began to swirl around him.

Misty was watching through the glasses. When Scooter finally started back, she handed them to her father with a frown. Tears were making flat tracks down Scooter's cheeks as he rode toward them on the pinto. The dogs picked up behind him. He came to them, then past them, wordlessly riding back the way they had come. Misty and her father followed, bewildered into silence by what they had just seen.

They rode for over twenty minutes before Scooter pulled up in the shelter of Picnic Rock and gestured for them to stop. "I'm in shock," he said tightly. "We have to find my dad." He rubbed his face with his hands. "That horse is worth thousands—maybe millions—of dollars. I can't imagine how my dad got him." He swallowed hard, took a deep breath, and said in a husky voice, "I know why he wanted him, though. He's what my ma always wanted—an Arabian with a bloody shoulder."

Misty and her father looked at Scooter in bewildered silence. They didn't even know what questions to ask.

"Unless I'm mistaken, and I'm sure I'm not, he's Mohit, the great-grandson of Ksiezna with the bloody shoulder and the son of Saheeh, arguably the most elegant Arabian that ever lived," Scooter paused, took a deep breath, then went on. "The last time I saw this horse, he was in southern California, on a posh horse farm outside Rancho de Oro—about 15 miles from where I live in La Jolla. That was two or three years ago. I'm a member of the International Arabian Horse Association, and I've been active for years in the California group that meets in San Diego. I'm usually invited to anything that has to do with Arabian horses. I've been to a couple of the fancy polo matches at the Cheval d'Básel Stables, and once, as a side event, they brought out some of their champion show horses. Mohit was the star."

"So, who owns the stable?" asked Misty's father.

"A French industrialist named Básel," replied Scooter. "Rumor was that he had paid over a million for Mohit. He was definitely the man's favorite pony. When I saw the horse last, he was being ridden by a trainer whose only job was to take care of that horse."

"Whoa," breathed Misty, and her father whistled softly in wonder.

"Let's go back to the house. I didn't find any papers about that horse when I looked through Dad's desk when I got home last night, but I'd like to look some more. I hope to heaven I find some." Scooter turned the pinto and trotted away with the wind. Soon, the three riders and the dogs were galloping toward the house.

When they rode into the yard, they saw Hooter taxiing down the road toward the ranch. There was no sign yet of the sheriff's helicopter.

"Misty, I'd appreciate it if you'd take care of the horses. I'll tell Ben to come and help you. Better unsaddle 'em. We may be here for a while." Misty's father gave her Sumo's reins, and Scooter led the pinto to her and gave her the reins.

"You can just put them in the barn," said Scooter. "There are plenty of empty stalls."

Misty led the sweaty horses behind Cadaver to the barn. In a few minutes, Ben came to help, but it was over an hour before they had finished with the horses and could return to the house. They found everyone in the side porch—a long room with a wall of windows, just off the kitchen. The Lawfords served meals there.

Scooter, their parents, the sheriff, Deputy Will, and Tony were grouped around a mammoth trestle table made of yellow pine that John Lawford had bargained for in Mexico over 40 years before. There were 20 chairs around the table—all different. All of them were pine, but each one was unique, and Scooter's father had a story for each chair. Kind of like the Lawford's horses, Misty thought—all of the same breed, but each so different. Misty sat down on one with a low back that she remembered Scooter's father had told her came from the old mission church in Lodgepole, not many miles from Littleville. It was an altar chair with a carved square back, a heavy square seat, and legs that were posted straight, Shaker style.

"Nope, we didn't see a thing," Tony was saying. He still wore his padded coveralls, and his ski -mask drooped over the rough buckskin upholstery that was hobnailed onto the back of the chair beside him. He grinned. "Had a great ride though."

The sheriff and his deputy had been there a bit longer. Their jackets were unzipped, and the coffee mugs in front of them were half empty. The sheriff was slumped in a sturdy, homemade arrow-back, and the deputy was leaning back in a clunky captain's chair.

Scooter brushed his hand over the top of his bristly hair, then rubbed his eyes. "Well, at least we're pretty sure my dad didn't go out on the ranch and run his pick-up off into a ravine or something." He looked at the sheriff. "Angela's going to help me go through the stuff in the house this afternoon, see if we can find anything around here that'll help us."

Sheriff Calahan stared into his coffee. "Well, like I said, we have all the alerts out. If anybody sees him, we'll hear about it." The sheriff trained his x-ray eyes on Hank and blinked as if he were sending Morse code. "I s'pose we better get on over and meet Jim McAndrews. Too bad he didn't pick up anything out of all those phone calls he made this morning."

"Nope, nobody'd heard from John," Hank said as he pushed back his big firehouse chair—one that had made the trip to the ranch strapped to the top of a horse trailer after a horse show in Chicago. He put his hand on Angela's back. "Why don't Misty and Tony stay here and help you? I'll fly Hooter back to the ranch. Ben can come with me. You all can bring the horses and the ATV when you come."

"O.K.," Misty's mother agreed. "I might even put them to work with a mop and a dust cloth. Looks like John hasn't had anybody in to clean for a while." She ran her hand across the top of the table, looked at the ashen strip of dust across her palm, and frowned at Scooter. "Would you mind?"

"Not hardly," Scooter said. "I was pretty appalled myself, when I got here. He used to have Alice Wheeler come in every week. Anybody have any idea why she hasn't been coming?"

No one responded. Angela shrugged her shoulders. Hank bent to give Angela a quick kiss, then he and Ben followed the Sheriff and Deputy Will out the door.

79

"I'll phone Claire and ask her to go over and get you some lunch, "Angela called out just before they pulled the door closed behind them. She looked at Scooter. "While we're looking, I'm going to start cataloging some of the stuff your dad's collected. He asked me to do that some time ago, and you should have a record of what's in this place."

Misty looked at Scooter. "So did you tell the sheriff about Mirage—er I mean Mohit?"

"I told the sheriff my dad had a new horse, but I didn't tell him where I'd seen him or anything about him," Scooter answered. "I thought I'd wait until we'd looked through the house and I'd had a chance to check my dad's safe deposit box at the bank—see if I can't find papers. I didn't want to raise a red flag until I know what's goin' on." Scooter turned to Angela and Tony and told them what he had discovered about his father's new horse.

Misty listened thoughtfully, then said said softly, "Well, whatever you might find, that horse is happy here. I hope this will always be his home—on this place—with your dad."

Chapter Nine

Angela and Scooter went to search in the rest of the house. Misty and Tony were assigned to the kitchen. Tony said they should search and clean at the same time. They began, following a plan artfully composed by Tony to get the most done in the least amount of time with the least energy expended. First they turned off the refrigerator, examined the contents, and dumped most of it into one of the giant-sized black plastic bags they found in big yellow boxes in the pantry. Then Misty sprayed the refrigerator with cleaner and scrubbed it down, leaving it turned off and the door propped open to allow it to air out. They did the same with the freezer, opening the packages, throwing out food that was past its use-by dates, some of it five years old. After the refrigerator and freezer, they cleaned the cupboards, dumping old containers of food and wiping out the drawers. They ran four loads of dishes through the dishwasher. It was after two o'clock when their mother came in to make some tea and called Scooter to join them.

They all flopped into chairs and sipped the tea as they ate nuts, toaster pastries, dried apricots, corned beef hash, chips and granola bars that Tony had foraged from the pantry. It seemed that Mr. Lawford purchased groceries by the crate. There were over six cases of different kinds of granola bars alone, and there were other boxes, cases of all kinds of food—soups, chips, coffee, crackers, popcorn—all kinds of snacks and sacks of pasta and dried foods—edibles that lasted for a long time and needed little preparation. Misty and Tony were especially impressed with the varieties of candy and nuts. These, according to the discount grocer's receipts taped on the boxes, had been purchased recently, probably within the past month or so. "Maybe he was stocking up for Halloween," Tony had joked.

"Why'd your dad buy so much food?" Misty asked Scooter when he came in to join them.

"Got me," Scooter replied. "Oh, we always did have a lot of extra on hand, because you never knew when you were going to get stuck out here, but I don't think I've ever seen *that* much stuff in the pantry."

"So how's it going with the rest of the house?" Misty asked. As they ate, she and Tony were playing tic-tac-toe in the dust that still coated the far end of the long table.

Their mother talked through the clasp she held in her mouth as she pulled her hair into a new plait at the back of her neck. "Well, I've been so busy cataloging, I haven't made much of a dent in the cleaning." She placed the clasp around the thick rope of hair and shook her head to make the clasp clear her collar. "This house is full of collector items, some of them antique, some of them just interesting. Some of them worthless, some of them pretty valuable. I wish I had my laptop though."

"And it's slow going in Dad's office," said Scooter. "I've found a lot of interesting stuff in the 'secret drawer' in his roll-top desk." When he said 'secret.' Scooter held up two curled fingers at the side of his face to indicate quotation marks. "I found the key taped to the bottom of another drawer. There were some papers on some of the other horses—Shadow, and even that brood mare I told you about,—the one he bought in Kentucky—but no papers on Mohit yet. I swear, my old man hasn't thrown anything away for at least ten years. If I weren't so concerned about the lease papers on that Arabian, I'd just dump it all into those trash bags and have a big bonfire."

"Doesn't he have a safe anywhere in the house?" Tony asked as he placed the final winning X in the corner of the tic-tac-toe matrix.

"Don't think so—at least he never told me about it if he does. He always put the working papers on his cattle and horses either in that hidden drawer in the desk or in an old Mexican saddlebag of his. Sometimes he'd take important papers in to his safe deposit box if he knew he wasn't going to need them for a while. We haven't found the saddlebag yet—it's buckskin leather with his name stitched on the flap. He always hid it somewhere, always changing where he put it, so no one else could find it, even though I never could figure out who else would be looking for it. Your mom's going to keep looking for it while she catalogs. I'm going to go to town pretty soon to see what's in the safe deposit box."

He looked at Tony. "Wanna go in with me? I could use your help. Thought I'd stop by Sandler's place and see if it was Dad that Misty saw there last Saturday—see if they know anything that might help. You know them better than I do."

Tony looked at his mother. "That O.K.?"

"This mess isn't going anywhere. Scooter could probably use some company," answered his mother.

"Can do," said Scooter. He looked at Tony. "Tell you what, we'll take that old white pickup that's in the shed. Probably hasn't been driven for quite a while, and we can load your ATV and take it home when we go."

The blue heelers watched mournfully from the end of the driveway as Scooter and Tony finally belched out of the yard in the rusty white truck. Misty watched them go, then turned on the radio to keep her company while she polished the dining porch furniture, swabbed the floor, and washed the windows.

When she was finished, she went to find her mother. Angela was sitting cross-legged in front of the bookcase in the living room with an assortment of silver plates, bowls, and goblets beside her. She was writing on a big yellow tablet.

"Gads, I'm glad they invented computers, and I wish I had mine," Angela said as Misty dropped down on the sofa above her. Her mother flexed her fingers, threw the tablet aside and lay down on her back on the thick wool Navajo rug. She pointed to some old guns with oversize barrels that were hanging on steel fingers, horizontally, above the stone fireplace.

"Know what those old guns are probably worth?" her mother asked.

"Haven't a clue," said Misty.

"Well, I saw one similar sell a couple of years ago for around $30,000. Old firearms aren't my area of expertise, but I'd bet each of those would go for more than that." She rolled over to face Misty and propped her head on her hand. "I've been telling John for years that he needed to insure those puppies or put them away, but he didn't seem to care. I guess his father traded a couple of Hereford bulls for them some years back."

Misty looked at her mother stretched out on the heavy rug. She was wearing old jeans and a sweatshirt. Angela was slender, but not thin, and she had a serpentine, unpredictable energy about her. Most people around the Sandhills thought her a bit scatter-brained and odd. Her freckled nose somehow made her seem less earnest than she was, and her hazel eyes held questions most of the time. Even when Angela was working at being stern, she seldom carried it off. That and her exaggerated concerns about her family had often made Misty feel the wiser of the two. In the past few months, however, she had come to realize that Angela wanted her to feel that way, that her mother had an insightful intelligence that helped her sort out what to give others in order to make them more sure of themselves. And she was a shrewd businesswoman. Misty knew it was her mother's antique trading that enabled her family to keep adding to the ranch.

"Aren't they insured?" Misty asked.

"Who knows. I should think they would fall under John's homeowner's policy, but if they haven't been appraised and catalogued, he'd have a hard time collecting," her mother replied. "It's been kind of spooky around here lately, and they never lock the doors. I think I'll hide them away before I leave. John can put them back up when he comes home."

Misty yawned. "I'm finished with the dining porch. What do you want me to do now?"

Misty's mom grimaced and looked up at her with eyes wide in fake horror. "I hate to do this to you, but would you mind attacking John's bedroom? I think Scooter already stripped the bed and picked up all the dirty clothes and dumped them in the laundry room. I've been keeping the washer running. At least that part's done, but Scooter said his dad's room's pretty awful."

Misty groaned. "I'll tell you what. I'll make lists in here, and you go clean the bedroom."

"Nope," her mother said, "you don't know what to look for, and from what I saw there's not that much important stuff in the bedroom. I'll come in there when I've finished here."

"What about the other bedrooms?" Misty asked.

"Haven't been used in years—except for the one Scooter slept in last night, and he said he whisked that up before he slept there. They're just dusty, that's all. I won't feel bad if they're not cleaned today."

"O.K." Misty pushed herself off the leather on the sofa. "Where's the vacuum?"

"Right behind you. I used it to get some of the dog hair off this rug," Her mother picked up her tablet, and exhaled heavily as she resumed her position in front of the bookcase.

Misty went to the kitchen and grabbed some of the cleaning cloths she had used in the dining porch, then wearily dragged the vacuum down the worn hall carpet to where her mother directed her: the first door on the left. She pushed on the heavy oak, and as the door opened, she wrinkled her nose at the stench. It smelled of manure, moldy fabrics, and sweat.

She stood in the doorway and yelled at her mother. "I'll bet Alice Wheeler never stepped foot in here. It's been a long time since anything's been done, that's for sure. Are you sure Mr. Lawford won't get mad if we clean his room?"

"Don't care if he does," Angela shouted back. "Never was like that when his wife was alive. We're going to clean in honor of Carolyn Lawford. Besides, it's not healthy for him to sleep in such filth."

"O.K." Misty stepped back, took a deep breath and pushed the vacuum into the room. She looked around, trying to decide where to begin. Mr. Lawford wasn't careless. The room was filled with things, but the clutter was carefully arranged.

Several stacks of magazines made towers along the wall by the bed—piles four and five feet high, leaning on each other for support. Misty walked over to look at the titles: *The Arabian Horse World, The Arabian Horse Times, The Arabian Finish Line*. More magazines about horses were in a ragged pile on the nightstand.

There were collections of things. Under the dressing table, there were five two-gallon ice cream buckets heaped full of coins—probably years of Mr. Lawford's pocket change. In one corner, pairs of worn cowboy boots, gray with dust, sagged companionably in an oversize laundry basket. Opposite the bed, there was a tall homemade cabinet. When she walked over to examine it, she found stacks of long-playing phonograph records with covers faded under a heavy

87

layer of grime. A dusty turntable with a plastic cover was on the top shelf. The bottom two shelves were stacked with what looked like scrapbooks or photo albums.

Looking around for something to sit on, since the filthy carpet wasn't very appealing, she saw a waist-high pile of balled-up quilts by the bed. She grabbed one off the side. Scooter had probably messed them up when he searched the room for the saddlebag. She folded it inside out and sat on it in front of the cabinet, frowning at the quilt's sour smell, and vowing to throw it in the washer when she got up.

After wiping off the cover of the book that was tilted on the top of the collection of albums, she turned it to the side; *Horus* had been written with a black marker in block letters down the spine. Holding her breath, she opened it carefully, ignoring her guilt and vowing to look no further if the contents were personal. A large, colored, somewhat faded photograph was inserted loosely at the front of the album. It was Carolyn Lawford—at least Misty assumed it was Mrs. Lawford: only her eyes and her hands could be seen. The rest of her body was covered by blue-turquoise chiffon, heavy jewels and silver braid. She was in full Arabic costume, and she was riding Horus.

The fine-boned gray-white horse with the melancholy eyes was princely in his black saddle and bridle which were heavily decorated with silver, sparkling glass, and tassels that matched his rider's veils and pantaloons. The horse and his rider were stunning. No wonder they were such a hit at horse shows. The banner in the back read CHEYENNE FRONTIER DAYS, but Misty couldn't make out the date.

Carefully, she turned to the pictures in the album; they were enclosed in transparent protectors that had become yellow and brittle. First a wary, weary, and very thin Horus on his first day at the ranch, his halter lead held by a slim, but obviously pregnant woman with a cloud of dark hair—Scooter's mom of course. A few pages back, a black and white snapshot of a man who looked something like Scooter, only with longer hair and sideburns—a young John Lawford—sitting bareback on a Horus whose health looked much improved. Halfway back, she found a picture of Horus rearing high on his back legs, and her stomach turned with excitement. His pose was exquisite in its arrogance, and the photograph had been taken from below, so it made the horse appear to be even more majestic. Misty wondered how the rider, Scooter's dad, managed to keep his place, since he had no saddle for support.

At the back of the album, there was a collection of ribbons and certificates. Horus had been a champion. Misty was sure that some of the silver cups, bowls and plates that were piled on the bookshelves where her mother was working had been given to honor this mystical stallion who looked as though he had just galloped out of a fairy tale.

"How're you coming?" Her mother shouted from the living room.

"Haven't started yet. Ran into some old scrapbooks," Misty answered, eager to look at the others as well.

"Well, why don't you clean first and look later. If, er *when,* Mr. Lawford comes home, our chance to do this is all over."

"O.K.," Misty said, frowning at her mother's slip of the tongue. For the first time, she considered that something might really have happened to their neighbor.

Reluctantly she replaced the scrapbook and started lifting off the other books, noting the names of the horses and peeking hastily at their pictures as she dusted. When she was finished with the albums, she went to the phonograph records and other keepsakes on the shelves, then on to the rest of the furniture. The mattress on the bed soon filled up with cans, cups, bags and bowls that held screws, books of matches, old business cards, receipts, combs, and anything else that John Lawford had happened to have in his pockets at the end of the day. She stacked them carefully in empty boxes she retrieved from the pantry and put them in the closet.

By the time her mother came in, Misty had wiped down all the furniture and was considering the waist-high heap of quilts in the corner. "How many dead cats do you suppose are under that pile of quilts?" Misty asked.

"I don't know, but we'd better move them, so you can clean this awful carpet. I'd like to rip the whole thing up."

The rug on the floor was stretched wall-to-wall and was matted and grime-shiny with dirt, so that it was difficult to tell what pattern or weave it had ever been. Angela grabbed a bedpost and rolled the castors of the heavy four-poster bed out of their nests and heaved the bed a couple of feet to the side. Underneath there was a thick layer of gray dust and mounds of dust balls, but they could tell that when the carpet when new it had been dark brown and shaggy, probably a very popular decorator item back about the time the Beatles were signing their first autographs for teenyboppers.

"O.K., let's move these quilts. I say let's just take 'em all to the laundry room." Angela grunted as she pulled three of them out, then said, "Ugh, they smell— and look at all that dog hair. Part of it looks like it came from Booster, remember him? He was the retriever John had about two dogs before the blue heelers." Angela left the room with a mound of quilts.

Misty started pulling at one of the comforters that made up the bottom layer. When she had it half way out, she noticed a corner of leather at the back. Excitedly, she pulled faster, thinking that perhaps she had found the saddlebag. But by the time her mother returned, she had thrown all the quilts into the hallway, and was standing over the bed where she had thrown a saddle and other tack on the bare mattress.

"Look what I found," she said.

Angela just stared at the brown leather in the middle of the bed, then slowly she walked over and bent to it, turning it over and examining the inside of the saddle. She peered to read the lettering on the inside of one of the flaps.

"I've never seen a saddle like that," said Misty.

"Neither have I," said her mother, "but I know what it is. It's an Arabian saddle—an *old* Arabian saddle." She turned it over and traced the designs around the edges of the side flaps and seat, stroking the silky leather, running her hand over the peak at the back and pinching the pad with her fingers. The girths lay on the bed beside the saddle. Angela picked them up—the long flat straps that were used to hold the saddle to the horse. These were about six inches wide. She smoothed out the stiff leather ties that were stitched to each end then gently rolled the soft, buttery leather of the strap between her thumb and forefinger.

"Well, there's not much to it, is there?" said Misty.

Her mother continued to stare at the leather between her fingers. "No, never has been. The Arabian saddles haven't changed much since the Arabs started using saddles—which was a very long time ago. Arabian saddles are not much more than a pad that curves to a peak at the back—and these…" She lifted the girths toward her daughter. "These are strapped around the horse so loosely that your dad said he always wondered how the rider stayed on."

"Well, there's a picture of Mr. Lawford down there." Misty nodded toward the albums. "He's riding that white Arabian called Horus that Scooter was talking about. The horse is straight up in the air, standing on his hind legs, and Mr. Lawford is riding bareback—he didn't even have a saddle. I wondered how he stayed on. Even *that* saddle would be better than bareback," said Misty.

"I wonder if Scooter knows this is here," Angela said irritably, as if to herself.

"I imagine. I'm pretty sure he went through the quilts looking for the saddlebag—at least they were all messed up. Why?" asked Misty.

Her mother hesitated, then answered in a slight Irish brogue that she used sometimes when she didn't want to sound too serious, "Misty Darlin', I could send ya through an Ivy League college with what that saddle would bring at auction at Christie's."

"You're kidding," said Misty.

"Nope," answered Angela. "I think I'll take this home with us for safe-keeping."

Chapter Ten

"Meanwhile back at the ranch…," Tony joked as he and Scooter pulled up beside the house at the Diamond W. There were seven pickups parked at random angles on the gravel drive. Three of them had large dogs in the beds sitting morosely with their heads hanging over the sides. They were either tied to their trucks or were obedient hounds that knew what it meant to "Stay!" The Diamond W's two black labs, Pinch and Scratch, bellowed dutifully when the white pickup approached, then, recognizing Tony when he jumped from the truck, went back to where they had been—lying on the ground watching the other dogs with careful brown eyes. Evidently the barking contest was over.

The sheriff's helicopter was sitting in the back by the horse barn.

"Looks like there's a party goin' on," said Scooter.

"The red one belongs to Jimmy McAndrews, the blue one is Larry Lopez's, and Ted Nolde drives the dark green short bed. The gray flatbad is Jimmy Hendren's dad's truck, and that shiny black 2500 with the big tires is Kevin Belle's. Let's see, I think the red and white one is Jimmy McAndrews' new hired man's. The old light green one is Steve Griese's."

"All of em border your dad's land?" asked Scooter.

Tony thought for a moment, then replied, "All but Hendren and Belle.

"Well, let's see what's goin' on," Scooter said as he slammed the door of the pickup.

"Kevin Belle's Mrs. Sandler's brother, y' know," Tony said as they walked toward the house, "but they don't get along. They say he works for one of those rich land grabbers. You ever see his place?"

Scooter shook his head.

"It's beautiful. Big barn and horse corrals. A white three-rail fence around the horse pasture. Looks like somethin' out of a magazine. Sheds all of his equipment."

"Not hard to figure out why he and Mrs. Sandler don't see eye to eye," said Scooter as he climbed the front steps.

Inside the house, the men were scattered about the big living room, mostly sitting with their hats in their hands and their arms propped on parted knees. Ben was leaning forward on the hassock in front of the fireplace. Only the sheriff was standing. No one was talking. Tony and Scooter nodded hello, and after Scooter was introduced to those he didn't know, he and Tony sat on opposite ends of the empty red kangaroo sofa. Evidently the other men had been reluctant to sit on such an exotic and feminine looking piece of furniture.

"I wish I knew how me an' Will could handle this," the sheriff said after a heavy sigh. "I think you can see from what I've told you that I just don't have the manpower to monitor this situation." He paused, his eyelids batting as he clenched his jaw. "I can file a report, I guess, but the only information you all have is that you can't find the cattle—and only part of this is in my jurisdiction. From what you're tellin' me, there's been rustlin' reported over an area that covers over 2,000 square miles. Figurin' 144 blocks to a square mile, that's over 288,000 city blocks. I figure there are about four county sheriffs' offices involved. Divide 288,000 by four and you get 72,000 city blocks apiece. That's a pretty big beat for any cop."

The sheriff turned and closed his stare onto Jimmy McAndrews, a slight, red-faced balding man who was staring straight ahead with his back erect and his hat on his knee. "I'm sorry, Jimmy, but me and the other lawmen have a lot a other things to do. We can't spend our time chasin' around the Sandhills every night."

There were a few more minutes of silence. Jimmy McAndrews started tapping his heel; some of the men turned their hats in their hands. Deputy Will blew his nose on a red handkerchief he took from his back pocket.

"Well Pilgrim," Ben said finally, in his best John Wayne imitation, "maybe it's time to call in the vigilantes."

Hank West scowled at Ben. "Hush, Ben, this is serious."

The sheriff set his steely eyes on Ben, blinked as though his eyelids were having spasms, then after a minute turned to Hank. "Maybe that's not such a bad idea, Hank. I don't mean like they used to do in Texas, taking the law into their own hands and hangin' folks and such—but maybe it's not such a bad idea for you all to start sort of a neighborhood watch—kind of like they do in the city."

"What do we do if we catch 'em?" Hank asked.

"Ya don't catch 'em, ya keep sight of 'em, and ya call me or one of the other law enforcement officers," said Sheriff Calahan.

Larry Lopez interrupted like a thunderclap. "I just wanta stop 'em." He was a tall, square-jawed man who moved slowly, but had a reputation for getting a lot done. "As I said before, this is a pretty nervy outfit stealin' those big yearlings. They must be takin' em across the state or to another branding area to sell 'em—or they'd couldn't get 'em to market—or else they're re-brandin' 'em and givin' the sale barn forged papers or some song and dance about havin' bought em off the original brander. They're professional rustlers. It's gotta stop."

In a calm voice, the Sheriff replied, "I'd say your best bet is to start lookin' out for them yourselves." He lifted each leg behind him and polished the shiny tips of his boots, one at a time, on the backs of his trousers. "Those rustlers aren't goin' to hang around here long if they know everyone in four counties is out for their hide, and you can alert the other ranchers if you see something that's out a line, maybe prevent a theft."

"That sounds good—lord knows I woulda liked to have had someone warn me, so I wouldn't a lost 20 of my best Angus, but how are we going to do that? There must be 50 ranchers we'd have to warn. It'd take a long time to call 50 people," said Ted Nolde.

"Well, we could set up a round-robin calling schedule—you know, I call Hank, he calls Larry, and so on…," said Jimmy McAndrews.

"But what if someone isn't home—or is out of town?" said Scooter.

"Could I make a suggestion?" Tony asked cautiously, looking at his father.

"Shoot," said Hank.

"How many of the ranchers do you think have e-mail?" asked Tony.

"A good share of 'em, I'd guess," said the sheriff.

"Well you could set up a mailing list with all the ranchers' e-mail addresses on it. All you would have to do is click on the name of that list, and it would go out instantly to everyone. If there's anybody who doesn't know how to do that, I could show them," said Tony carefully, trying to be helpful, and at the same time, trying not to irritate any of the men by seeming too clever. He went on. "If some of the ranchers don't have computers yet, they could get one of those keyboards that hook up with a television set and subscribe to an e-mail service through that. They only cost about $100. We could even encrypt the messages, send them in a code that could only be broken by the receiver's computer. Then the crooks couldn't' hack in and find out what we know."

All the men in the room studied Tony. No one spoke for about a minute, then Steve Griese, a stocky man with petroleum black hair and ruddy skin said, "Ya know I've been tryin' to avoid computers 'bout every day for the last three-four years." He looked sideways at Hank. "Oh, we have one. The kids use it, and I check the markets and play games on it, but I never thought we'd be thinkin' of usin' computers to catch rustlers."

"Well, you'd have to make sure you check your e-mail regularly, and I'd suggest you go one step further and make sure everyone has a GPS. That way when you do give the Sheriff or the other ranchers any information about the location of a suspicious activity, they can pinpoint exactly where you're talking about." Tony spoke slowly and carefully.

Scooter tried hard to suppress a grin. He could see that Hank was comfortable with what Tony was suggesting, as were Ted Nolde, Carl Hendren, and maybe Steve Griese—men who had children who were raised with computers. The other men in the room were trying hard not to be annoyed.

Most of them owned the technology and surfed the net occasionally, used it to check the weather and the price of hay. But they were men of nature, men who came to ranching or stayed in ranching because they wanted to use their hands and hearts to make a living off the land. For the most part they stayed in the Sandhills because they loved the animals and the freedom—finding old arrowheads in the sand, watching a flock of sandhill cranes return to the lakes in the springtime, and the smell of the air before a rainstorm.

They didn't want to take the time to learn how operate something that kept them confined to a desk, and they didn't want to be any more dependent on technology than they already were. They were frustrated daily by cellular telephones whose signals were made fickle by the quirky, sand-filled breezes of the Nebraska hill country. They resented the computer-designed chemicals they had to buy to keep

99

their stock healthy and the Canada thistle out of their pastures. They were worn down by satellite television systems with remote controls so complicated, that pushing one wrong button could mean ten minutes wasted trying to get the picture back on the screen. And now, they had to tie themselves to technology in another way.

"How are we going to go about getting all the other ranchers to get on board with this?" asked Steve Griese.

Tony knew his allotted portion of conversation in this group had been overspent, so he kept quiet.

Jimmy McAndrews leaned forward. "My wife works at the courthouse. She can get the names and addresses. I'll write a letter; a couple of you guys can check it over to see if I covered everything, and we'll mail 'em out on Monday. We'll tell everyone what we have in mind and ask for everyone's e-mail address. I'll even buy the stamps. I wanna get this thing stopped."

"That's the plan, then," said Larry Lopez, and the other men rose in silent agreement. After a few minutes of small talk, they began to shuffle toward the door.

Scooter put his hand on Kevin Belle's arm as the big man crossed in front of him. "Mr. Belle."

"Yes." Kevin Belle turned toward him. He was a tall, heavy and slope-shouldered man with light blue eyes and a square face like his sister's. His blue jeans were pressed, and his shirt looked new.

"Could I talk to you for a minute?" asked Scooter.

"Sure can," said Kevin. "You know I'd be happy to be a captain or something. Since I'm a bachelor, I have a little more free time than some of the other ranchers." He had a deep, musical voice, perfect diction, and an open manner. The way he spoke reminded Tony of a network television newscaster.

"Well, you can talk to Hank about that. I wanted to ask you about something else," said Scooter.

"Shoot," said Kevin Belle.

"As Hank might have told you, my dad hasn't reported in for a couple of days, and we don't know where he is."

Kevin Belle nodded, turning his hat in his hands as he listened.

"Somebody said they saw his pickup at your sister's house a few days ago. I thought she might know something. I went to see her, but she wasn't home—looked like she hadn't been there in a while. Do you know how I could reach her?"

Kevin stared at Scooter, then looked over at Tony and Hank before he spoke. "I'm sure someone around here has told you that my sister doesn't like me much any more. I would be the last person to know where she is." He shook his head. "I love her, and I love those kids, but she won't talk to me. I'm sorry it's that way, but that's just the way it is."

"I'm sorry," said Scooter.

Kevin nodded. "She's a willful and hard-headed woman." He turned to Hank. "Let me know if there's anything else I can do to help."

"If you're willing to do something extra for the cattle watch, tell Jimmy," said Hank. Kevin nodded

and left the house. Soon they could see him leaning
against Jimmy McAndrews' pickup, talking with him.

"Belle seems like an O.K. sort," said Scooter.

Hank nodded. "A good neighbor and smart as hell.
His liberal sister doesn't like him much though."

The telephone rang. Hank rose to answer it.

"O.K., Hon, that sounds like a smart thing to do."
Scooter, Tony and Ben listened to Hank's end of the
conversation. "O.K., I'll tell him." A pause to listen,
then, "Yeah, Hooter's in the hangar. I refueled her."
and then, "Nope, nothin' from John. A lot's gone on
here, but nothin' that can't wait til you get home. You
and Misty drive careful." A pause, then, "Just a
minute." He turned to Scooter. "You want Angela
and Misty to leave the pinto in the barn? He's fed."

"Yeah, he'll be O.K." Scooter said.

"That'd be fine, Hon. See ya soon." Hank hung up
the phone. "Angela said they were comin' home.
She'll fly over tomorrow and catalog the rest. They
hid those old muskets your father had hangin' above
the fireplace. They're in a bunch of bedding in a closet
at the back of one the upstairs bedrooms. Said with
strangers around, it didn't seem smart to leave them
out in the open. Said she's bringin' a saddle home—
one they found in John's bedroom under some quilts.
Doesn't feel right leavin' it there with everything that's
goin' on."

Scooter nodded. "I ran into that saddle when I was
looking for the saddlebag. It was under some old
quilts in my dad's bedroom. You remember that
saddle, Hank. That thing's been around ever since I
can remember. My dad bought it in Seattle years ago.

Said it originally belonged to some Egyptian prince who was a real fanatic about Arabian horses."

"Yeah, your dad told me that story," said Hank. "Said that in the early 1900's, the guy was in the states, showing his horses when his father died, and it was his turn to be king, and he wasn't so anxious to do that."

"The prince refused to take the throne," said Scooter, "And for a while, until his brother agreed to be crowned, they cut him off, and he had no money. He had to sell the saddle and one of his horses to get back home, left a hell of a hotel bill." Scooter tilted a slight smile on one side of his face.

"Well, she thinks it's pretty valuable—the guns too. Maybe I should have told her to lock up the house," said Hank.

"Nah, anybody wants to get in, they'll get in; a lock won't keep them out," said Scooter.

"You're probably right," said Hank, "but I think Angela was right to bring the saddle. She has a big safe bolted in the back of the Land Rover. She's gonna put it in there when she gets home. No sense in leavin' that stuff right out in the open. She said she stuck a couple of pieces of driftwood up there where the guns were."

Scooter nodded, then added, "Obviously she didn't hear from my dad while she was over there—and Tony and I came up dry. The safe deposit box was empty except for my dad's will and some other old deeds and life insurance papers. Hard to tell how long the Sandlers had been gone, the place is always such a mess. Looked to me like the pile of junk around their house had spread out about 50 yards each way since the last time I was there."

"Yeah." Hank took a handkerchief out of his back pocket and covered his nose as he sneezed, again, and again. "Damned allergies." He sniffed, then took a deep breath. "The Sandler place got worse while she was fightin' to save those boys. I guess collectin' things made her feel better." He paused, then went on. "She just about pounded down everyone in the county tryin' to make everybody see those two rascals were innocent. It was kind of a losin' battle though. Everyone around had seen those boys comin' and goin' from that potato cellar on the other end of their section, and they were caught red-handed in that meth lab."

Scooter nodded with a frown. "And meth is truly terrible stuff. As a physician, I can tell you that some of the brain scans on habitual users of methamphetamines show their brains have actually been physically changed by the stuff. They've allowed the drug to eat away at their memories and their personalities. I can't imagine why people would purposely destroy themselves like that. Did they catch the boys selling it?"

"They never caught 'em sellin', never caught em usin'. I play golf with the judge—he said they coulda been workin' with a dope ring, but those boys wouldn't admit anything, and they didn't finger anybody." Hank blew his nose and wiped his eyes. "I guess that's not unusual though; I hear those dopers usually stick pretty close. Judge told me they know they stand to get hurt or killed if they talk," said Hank.

"I think they put those boys away for a coupla years at least."

"Good," said Scooter.

The big mahogany grandfather clock in the hallway that had been keeping time since the early 1800's began six sonorous gongs.

Ben stood up. "That reminds me. I'm hungry. How 'bout I thaw some steaks for us to grill when Mom gets home?"

"Sounds good," agreed his father.

Tony got to his feet. "I'll fix some cheese dip and crackers to tide us over."

Chapter Eleven

"Are you sure you want to drive all the way home, Scooter? It's almost 9:00. We have an extra bed in Tony's room," said Angela.

They were sitting around the table drinking tea and coffee. Bare T-bones and empty potato skins were cold on their plates.

Scooter sighed. "Ah, I don't know. I just feel I should be back at home in case Dad calls—or someone calls about him."

"But I forwarded all your calls before I left your place, so they would ring in here," Angela reminded him.

"Yes, I know, but for some reason I just feel I ought to be at home," Scooter said.

"I understand. I'd probably feel the same way," said Hank. "You're sure welcome to stay here though."

"Well, let me check my service, see if anything has come in during the past couple of hours." Scooter pushed his chair back from the table and walked to the telephone in the hallway.

Angela started gathering the plates off the table; she turned to Misty. "Hon, since I'm going back over to Lawford's in the morning, would you and one of the boys go into Kilpatrick for me to pick up the dry cleaning and run some other errands?"

Misty rose to help. "Sure, we can do that." She looked at the boys. "Who wants to go?"

"Well, I was kinda planning on going over to help the Nolde's round up some calves," said Tony.

Ben rolled his eyes. "Boy, all you have to do to get free help is to have a good-lookin' daughter."

Hank grinned. "Kind of a fair trade, I'd say. Lono's been over here at branding, and you've seen her, she always holds her own and then some."

"Boy, all you have to do to get free help is to have a geeky son," Ben said dully. "I'll go with you, Misty. I need some new jeans. I ripped my only good pair when I jumped out of the plane today. And we need to get Scratch a new collar. He's lost another one diggin' for rabbits somewhere."

Scooter returned to the dining room as they were clearing the last of the dishes from the table. "Well, I heard from him," he said, shaking his head. "Called and left a message to tell me he's been in New Mexico, visiting an old friend, Jackie Campbell. You know Jackie, Hank?'

Hank shook his head with a frown.

"She's been around longer than my dad," Scooter continued. "She keeps a horse farm down by the Pecos river—mostly Spanish-bred Arabians. Dad said he was on his way home—wondered when I was coming to visit. I guess at least part of the mystery's solved, but he didn't say when he'd be home. I got Jackie's number from information and tried to reach her, but I just got an answering machine. Left her a message, asking her to get in touch with me. If she gets back to me, maybe she can tell me when to expect him."

"Well, that's a relief," said Angela as she headed for the kitchen with a stack of dirty plates.

"Sure is," said Hank.

"It's still kind of weird, him takin' off without telling anyone, and forgetting I was coming in this weekend," said Scooter.

"Well, sometimes when you live alone, you don't worry about reportin' in—and I've been known to forget an engagement or two," said Hank with a half-grin.

"I don't know," said Scooter. "I think I will go on back to the ranch, though—in case he does come home, and I'll just feel better if I'm at the house if he calls again."

"Well, don't forget to cancel the forward I put on your phone," Angela yelled from the kitchen.

"I won't," said Scooter, "and thanks to all of you for everything you're doing to help me and my dad."

"Happy to help," said Hank.

"Happy to have an excuse to get your dad's house back in order," grinned Angela from the kitchen-dining room door. "You take care now, and call us in the morning.

In a few minutes, they heard the stubborn roar of the white pickup's old engine, and their guest left for home.

Hank stopped Ben as he started downstairs to watch television. "Why don't you take that bag phone and get it fixed when you and Misty go into Kilpatrick tomorrow. It's in the bottom drawer of the filing cabinet in my office."

"O.K.," said Ben. "Might have to trade it in—don't see how they can fix it."

"Well, do what you have to do," his father said and handed Ben his credit card.

The next day was a gold and brown October Saturday. Misty and Ben ate oatmeal with their mother, then watched out the window as the dogs barked and scrambled in front of the Range Rover, ushering Angela to the hangar to get Hooter. Ben retrieved the damaged cell phone from the filing cabinet, and soon he and Misty had buckled themselves into their father's black Jeep.

Once out of the yard, Ben inserted a CD, an album cut by his favorite heavy metal group, *Bottled Water*. Then he slid the volume control to a place just short of its highest position, buzzed the back of his seat to a reclining position, removed his boots, and beat time on the dash with his toes. "How long we goin' to be in town?" Ben shouted over the electric guitars.

Misty pushed down on the sliding volume adjustment. "Well, I kind of promised Danny I'd have lunch with him at the new barbecue place. Wanna come?" Misty looked sideways at Ben.

He shook his head, "Nah, I'll do the honors with the cell phone. On Saturdays, Cellservice is always so busy it'll probably take an hour. I'll go over to Taco De Oro next door when I'm through, and you can pick me up there." He sat up to boost the volume of the stereo, then he turned up the base and lay back in the seat again with his feet on the dash. He kept time to the music with his upper body and sang along, "I bang my head (beat, beat, beat), I rang my head (beat, beat, beat), I hang my head (beat, beat, beat), I feel like lead (beat, beat, beat, beat, beat, beat)."

109

When Misty finally turned off the engine after she parked the car in front of a bustling discount store in Kilpatrick, the silence was almost eerie. "An hour of *Bottled Water* is truly a life-changing experience," she said as she reached into the back seat to get her purse.

"Yeah, kind of gets ya right here doesn't it?" Ben pounded on his chest with one fist.

"Gives silence a whole new dimension," she answered.

"Theeeeer'es Slick," Ben said. He pushed the door out, stood up, perched on the doorframe and leaned over with his arms resting on the top of the open door.

"Hey Slick!" he yelled.

Danny McFarland waved from the other side of parking lot. He was waiting for cars to pass, so he could walk toward them. He, like Ben and Tony, was not far from six-feet tall and still growing. Wrap-around sunglasses sat on his wide nose and covered his blue eyes. A black and red football jersey with a bold "N" on the front hung on his lanky body over baggy, faded jeans. Since he had shaved his head at the beginning of football season, his head was a brush of dark fuzz.

"Ben, please," said Misty. "Come on."

"O.K." He jumped down, closed the door and dodged between cars to get to the entrance of the store. He strutted up and down on the sidewalk with his hands in his pockets until Misty and Danny joined him there.

"You guys are so slow. Come on, I've got shopping to do." Ben pushed the door open and led them inside.

Misty and Danny followed with good-natured indulgence.

It was after two o'clock when Misty pulled up in front of Taco De Oro. Danny was in the passenger seat beside her. They could see Ben near the front window of the restaurant, his feet propped on the seat of the chair beside him. He was talking with a man who was sitting across the table eating his lunch. When Ben saw Misty, he stood, shook hands with the man, and came out of the restaurant carrying a small shopping bag.

Misty rolled down her window. "Sorry we're so late. It took longer at the mall than I thought it would."

"Yeah, sure, I'll bet," said Ben as he hopped into the back seat. "I'll bet you and Slick were out by the lake playin' kissy face."

"Huh, I wish—," said Danny. "Your sister dragged me around to every store in town. Wouldn't let just *any* woman do that."

"Well, let's go," said Ben. "Time's awastin'."

"Did you get the phone fixed?" Misty asked as she was backing away from the restaurant.

"Couldn't fix it. Had to get a new one," said Ben. "They gave me a big discount, though."

"Did they have any kind of a guess as to how it got damaged?" asked Misty.

"Sorta. Did you see that big guy I was talking to in the restaurant?" asked Ben.

"Yeah," said Danny. "He runs Cellservice doesn't he?"

"Sure does," Ben said. "His name is Bob Garcia. The girl who waited on me in Cellservice showed him the phone, needed his say-so before she could make a decision about how to handle it. He was kind of interested, asked me about it. Then when he came into the restaurant, he was tellin' me that the cord that was cut has double insulation to prevent interference and extra heavy wire—no way it was an accident. Someone used wire cutters to deliberately disable the phone."

"Well, that's pretty much what we thought," said Misty.

Danny turned to talk to Ben in the back seat, "Misty told me about the horse, the Hummers and all. I promised her I wouldn't say anything to anyone. Pretty wild." He turned back to Misty. "How 'bout I come out next week-end to see that horse? I'd come tomorrow, but I have to work." Danny worked part-time at one of the local supermarkets—bagging groceries and carrying them to customers' cars.

"Sure, if Scooter says it's O.K.—or Mr. Lawford, if he's home," said Misty.

They delivered Danny to his Jeep; Ben did a flip into the front seat, and they were back on the highway—headed toward the Diamond W.

"So how much have you told Slick about what's happened during the last coupla days?" asked Ben.

"Not everything," said Misty, "Just that Mr. Lawford has a beautiful horse, that we saw the Humvees, and that our phone cord was cut. He promised not to talk to anyone about any of it, because, after all, there may be a perfectly logical explanation for everything—and I wouldn't want everyone talking."

"Yep, don't wanta feed the gossip mills." Ben turned his cap around, so the bill was in the front, returned his seat to a reclining position, pulled his hat over his eyes, crossed his arms on his chest and within minutes was snoring loudly. Misty couldn't decide which was worse: *Bottled Water* or Ben's snoring—for which he was notorious among his family and friends. When he went camping with his buddies, they usually made him sleep in a tent by himself—and Tony had banished him to another bedroom years ago. Misty inserted one of her mother's jazz discs and turned up the volume to drown out the glottal sounds coming from the passenger seat.

They were approaching *Juniper State Park*, a wildlife refuge about 10 miles east of Kilpatrick, when Misty reached over and shook Ben's arm. "Hey, wake up!" Misty said abruptly.

"What's up?" he asked. Ben raised the bill of his hat and sat up in the seat. It always amazed Misty that Ben could be sleeping soundly, but if you woke him, he was fully awake in no more than a second.

"Look, ahead there," she said. A bi-level cattle truck with a long bed was pulling across the highway, coming out of the entrance to the park. They slowed to give it plenty of time to make the turn. As they passed it, they could see there was a woman driving the tractor of the truck and that the bed was empty of cattle. It had a commercial license plate issued in Kansas. Ben read the number aloud.

"That's weird. What would a cattle truck like that be doing in the park?" said Misty.

"Maybe they wanted to go into the Visitor's Center," said Ben.

"It closed the first of October," said Misty. "Besides, it's on the other side of the road."

"Maybe she had a long way to drive and needed a nap," said Ben, "or the obvious, maybe she wanted to make a puddle behind a pine tree."

"Yeah, that could be it, and ordinarily, I wouldn't think anything about it, but since we're supposed to be doing this neighborhood watch thing, what say we just drive into the park to see if we see anything?" Misty slowed the SUV.

"My time is your time," said Ben.

Misty turned into a shallow drive, backed onto the shoulder of the highway, and headed back the other way.

At the entrance, she turned to follow the gravel road into the park.

"Lemme out, and I'll check for tracks. We should be able to tell where the truck came from." Ben jumped from the SUV, closed the door, and then hopped up on the fender on the passenger side. He motioned for her to go forward. They drove slowly for another twenty minutes, winding their way deep into the park before Ben signaled for her to stop and vaulted to the ground. Once there he pointed to a spot behind a big boulder and put his finger to his lips to caution her to be quiet.

Misty closed her door softly and came around so she could see what he was pointing at. They peered through some bushes at the side of the boulder. A ways down, on a flat spot in the valley, there was a camp-stove for cooking and two mud-colored, dome-shaped tents. Ben took her head with his hands, turned it, and pointed to another site to the left and under some brush. There lay a dead Simmental yearling—a spotted skewbald, speckled white and red. He had the big head with a long face and large ears set low—characteristic of his breed. The head was stretched up and at an unnatural angle just like the oreo calf Tony had found on the Diamond W. Ben thought to himself that this calf would weigh in close to 1,000 pounds—not an animal that would be easy to overcome—or to hide.

Ben took off his red jacket, gave it to Misty and signaled for her to get back in the Jeep. He lay down on the ground and snaked across the open area between the boulder and a clump of trees. Once there, he examined the ground then walked for a few yards to the other side of the trees. After a few minutes, he reappeared and wiggled back across to hide behind the boulder. After he watched below for a few minutes more, he returned to the Jeep. "Get out of here and be quiet as you can. I'm glad we've got this buggy instead of one of the noisy pickups."

Misty started the big vehicle and backed up very slowly until she reached a small open spot where she could turn around.

"They've had Humvees down there. I found tracks." Ben said.

Ben reached back to get the new bag phone, plugged it in, and as soon as it beeped, signaling that it was operable, Ben dialed home.

"Hi Dad, Gees, I'm glad you're home. Misty and I just ran into something." He explained to his father what they had just seen, and then he listened for a moment. "No, I didn't have Sheriff Calahan's direct number. Didn't wanta just call 911." Pause. "O.K. D'you want us to wait?" Pause. "O.K. Tell him to go into the park on the south side, go three miles south, two west, turn right at the pond and follow the trail around the ridge. There's a big boulder there. The camp's just below to the right; the calf was just up and left of there." Pause. "You got it," Ben said. "Yeah, this phone has the same number as the other one." Pause. "We're on our way." To Misty, he said, "He wants us to come home. He's going to get the Sheriff in here."

Carefully, but as fast as she dared, Misty drove back through the park. At the exit, she turned with relief onto the highway and headed for home. About a mile before they were to make the turn off the highway to head down the county road to Stoop's Corner, they heard the Sheriff's siren. They pulled to the shoulder of the highway, and the Sheriff's white car went by in a blur toward Juniper Park. Just after that, the bag phone rang.

"Ben, your dad didn't say what color that cattle truck was." It was Sheriff Calahan.

"The front, the tractor, was dark blue. The back was gray metal, had no paint," Ben answered carefully.

"And a commercial license out of Kansas, right?"

"Yes, number J5-134."

O.K., thanks. You kids get on home now." the sheriff broke the connection.

As they were pulling into the yard at the Diamond W, the cell phone rang again.

"Ho," said Ben.

"Ben, I can see where they were camped, and I can see where they drug that calf, but they're not here anymore. Must a seen you and Misty and got spooked. We'll collect what we can though. Don't like it that that they might have seen your car and might know who you are. You kids be careful," growled the Sheriff.

"What about the license plate?" asked Ben.

"Stolen about a month ago—from a truck that was parked in a truck stop in Wyoming," said the sheriff. "How close to home are you?"

"Just pulled into the yard," Ben said.

"Well stay there," growled the sheriff. "Tell your folks and Scooter what we found. I'll call 'em later."

Chapter Twelve

Their father was tipped back in his chair talking on the telephone when they walked into his office. "It *is* funny that Scooter hasn't heard from him again—and you say the woman in New Mexico hasn't gotten back to him." Hank paused to listen to his wife. "Well, there's really not much he can do here." Pause. "The kids just walked in. I'll put you on speaker." Hank looked at Misty and Ben. "What happened?" he asked.

Misty and Ben took turns relaying what they had learned from the sheriff.

"Scooter's going back to California this afternoon." Their mother's voice came over the speakerphone. "A plane is flying into Kilpatrick to pick him up in about an hour. His office called; he has to give someone a new eye tomorrow, and he says while he's back there, he wants to see what he can find out about that Arabian. He hasn't been able to find out anything over the telephone; all the numbers are unlisted." After a moment, she added, "He was wondering though if we couldn't check on the horse—make sure he's O.K."

Misty looked at Ben, then at their father.

"Sure, we can do that, Hon," said Hank. "We'll come over in a bit. I'll call Tony and tell him to stay at Nolde's."

"Oh, he'll hate that," Ben said sarcastically.

Before long, they were in the big red pickup with the stretch cab. Ben was spread out on the bench seat behind his father and Misty. As they drove the rough back road to Lawford's, an autumn breeze drew up behind the hills and grew steadily stronger. Hank cursed as the wind sucked up the prairie dust and blew it in shadowy sheets across the road. By the time they pulled into the Lawford's yard, his eyes were red and swollen and tears were running down his cheeks. He blew his nose and sneezed several times in succession.

"Damned allergies," he said in low, yet squeaky, voice. "I forgot my medicine. I don't have any business out here with that dust blowing. You kids'll have to check the horses."

"We can do that," said Ben. "Shouldn't take long if they're still over in the hills where they were the other day."

"Well, go on then. The afternoon's gettin' along. I'll explain it to your mother. And take the phone. If you don't find'em in half an hour or so, give a ring, and your mom or I will come out in Hooter and try to spot'em for ya," said his father.

Misty motioned for Ben to get behind the wheel. He was a much better driver than she was when they were off-road. Ben's exceptional eyesight, quick reaction time, intuitive sense of space, and natural grace made him seem to become a part of whatever vehicle or animal he happened to be depending on for transportation. But his confidence and ability took him to places most people wouldn't go. Misty knew that with Ben driving they would go over ruts and bumps and have more than a few surprise bounces—that there would be times when he would take her breath away. She got in the passenger seat, buckled her seat belt, pulled her hat down tightly on her head. Then after taking a deep breath, she clutched the swinging handle on the roof above the door and closed her eyes. Ben slid into the driver's seat, slammed the door shut, buckled his seat belt, and with a growl, shifted into low gear. They were on their way.

Ben took the pickup over the same route they had taken on the horses the day before—exactly the same route—only at much faster speeds. Never mind that there were large yuccas scraping the bottom of the truck or that he had to veer at right angles to avoid massive rocks and deep ruts. Never mind that they plowed through soft sand that made their vehicle swerve and shiver until it was back on firm ground again. The pickup went around, over, through, and into—until they pulled up beside the bluff where they had spotted the horses two days before. Misty peeled the fingers on her right hand from the handle on the roof and exhaled. Stiffly, she unbuckled her seat belt and opened her door. Ben was already out of the truck, standing in the bed of the pickup using the binoculars to scan the narrow valley.

"Don't see 'em," he said. "Wish Mr. Lawford would have fenced his pastures off a little more. Sure would make it easier to keep track of his herd." He jumped out of the back of the truck and walked around until he was at the apex of the outcropping of the bluff. He kneeled and leveled the glasses to look for the horses.

"That may be them over by that far windmill," he said loudly. He jumped off the rock and opened the door to the pickup. "Let's go see," he said.

After another 15-minute ride over untamed prairie, they were at the windmill. There were no horses, and clouds were covering the sun. It was unnaturally dark for a late afternoon in October.

"I'm going to call Dad," Misty said as she picked up the handset of the cell phone. Her father answered after one ring.

"Find em?" he asked.

"Not yet," Misty answered. "We're clear out on the north side, sort of in the middle of the top of the mushroom, I think."

"Well, I was just watching the weather channel. There may be some rough weather coming. I don't think we want to take Hooter out. I think you two better head back here. We'll find the horses in the morning," her father's words were muffled in the throaty bypass of his stuffy nose.

"Just a minute," said Misty. She turned to Ben. "He says to come home," she said firmly.

"Can't see what else we can do," Ben agreed.

"We're on our way," said Misty, and she replaced the handset in the cradle that rested in the leather bag.

They turned the pickup around and proceeded at a somewhat less heart-stopping pace back the way they had come. By the time they reached Apple Rock, the clouds were dark, and the smell of rain was in the air.

Ben stopped the pickup abruptly.

"Just a minute," he said. He bounded out of the truck and scaled up the slope of the sandstone landmark. He sat hunched at the top, oblivious to the heavy drops of rain that had begun to splatter on the dry clay. Finally, he slid, then jumped to the ground and returned to the shelter of the pickup. He started the motor, checked the windshield wipers, and then swung the pickup around to climb to the top of a long, narrow hill. Once there, he parked and picked up the binoculars.

"Do you see that light over there?" he pointed to the far right.

Misty squinted in the direction in which he was pointing. There was a glow against the clouds.

"I think I do," she said. "What is it, aurora borealis?" She was referring to the luminous bands of light often seen in the hills, thought to be caused by some sort of electrical charge in the magnetic fields of the north.

"I don't think so. I think it's artificial light—has that yellow-gray glow about it," Ben said softly. "I'm going to take the ATV down there."

"I think you'd better call and ask Dad first," said Misty. "It's getting pretty dark, and it's raining."

"I'm just going to sneak down there and take a look, won't take but a few minutes. The wind's coming from that direction, so if there is anybody down there, they shouldn't hear me."

Ben pulled the hood of his windbreaker out of the pouch at the back of his neck and tied it tight about his head, and then he slammed out of the pickup. Soon Misty heard the bang of the tailgate and the scrape of metal as he put down the ramp so he could drive the four-wheeler down from the bed of the truck. Next came the put-put-put of its engine, and she could feel the bed of the truck raise as Ben drove the golf-cart-size vehicle with the big heavy tires onto the ground.

She picked up the handset of the bag phone as Ben pulled around past her window and started down the hill. Her mother answered after the first ring.

"Ben decided to make a quick trip cross-country with the ATV," said Misty, "so we may be delayed a few minutes getting home."

"Why on earth is he doing that?" asked her mother.

"He saw something in the valley, and he wanted to see what it was," Misty replied evasively, "He won't be gone for long, I'm sure."

"What did he see?" asked her mother.

"Got me," said Misty, "he just took off." She was reluctant to worry her mother about some mysterious lights that would very likely turn out to be a natural phenomenon.

"Is it raining there?" Angela asked with worry in her voice.

"Yeah, some rain with lots of wind. No thunder or lightening though," Misty said.

"Ben should have called before he took off," replied her mother.

"Yes, I know, but he said he'd be gone for just a bit," sighed Misty. "You know how hard it is to stop him when he's decided to do something."

"How well I know," replied her mother. "Just a minute."

Misty could hear her mother explaining the situation to her father.

"Your father says to get back in here as soon as you can," Angela said when she came back on the line.

"We will," Misty said and pushed the End Call button.

Even though it was almost dark, Ben was churning down the hillsides without his headlights. If there was someone around the place where he had spotted the lights, he didn't want them to know he was there. As he got closer, he became convinced that the glow was coming from headlights or spotlights of some kind. He decided to circle around a big bank in the prairie, so he could come up on the side and have a better view. Painstakingly, going slowly and without revving the motor, he guided the four-wheeler between small prairie swells at the edge of the knoll, so he would be less likely to be seen.

He was just short of his destination when the vehicle lurched sideways down the side of the hill into a wide, v-shaped rut. One of the front wheels buried itself in the wet sand, and in slow motion, the ATV tipped over into the hole. Before it hit the ground, Ben had jumped from his seat. Disgusted, he kneeled in the damp dirt to examine the wheels to see what he would have to do to free the rugged tractor-car, but just as he stood up to look about for something he could use for a shovel, someone grabbed him from behind.

Strong arms pinned him about the waist, taking his breath away, as another pair of hands slipped a heavy black plastic bag loosely over his head and in one motion, taped it firmly, but not tightly around his neck. He didn't struggle; his instincts told him to remain docile as his arms were pinned back, and plastic cuffs were clipped around his wrists. He was sure that fighting back would only get him hurt. Both of the men seemed to take up a lot of space. The arms of the first man, and the hands of the second, were bulky and muscular. His capture seemed a casual task for them.

"Who are you, and what are you doin'?" Ben's question was muffled by the plastic. One of the men stabbed small holes in the back of the bag, so he would get fresh air. Neither of the two said anything. They weren't even breathing hard. They stood away from him. He couldn't hear them, he couldn't see them, and he couldn't feel them.

He heard the sound of a heavy motor then, and soon after it stopped, he was completely surprised when they kicked his feet out from under him. They taped his ankles together and rolled him onto a shallow trailer where they tied his hands and feet to the sides. The men didn't get into the truck that was pulling the flatbed, nor did they seem to be in the back with him. Evidently someone else was behind the wheel. The driver gunned the motor, and the engine groaned as the truck and trailer made their way across the bumpy prairie.

Ben was getting damp from the rain, but he was sure his feet inside his Tony Lama boots were soaking wet, because was he more afraid than he had ever been in his life. He thought back to the Polish boy who had been trapped under the horse trailer. Ben felt sick. Now he knew what it was like to be so completely helpless.

Chapter Thirteen

Ben tried to cushion his head on his arm to protect it as they bumped across the hills. His legs were cramped, his hip and side were getting sore from being tossed about on the flat bed of the open trailer, and he was soaked from the rain. It seemed to Ben they were going in circles, but the driver would stop periodically, get out, and throw something into the back of the trailer. When they finally stopped for good, he realized his body was trembling from bracing himself against the steel railings of the trailer bed.

He heard the driver leave the truck, then he heard a vehicle grinding toward them, and in a few minutes, another came. Their motors had the same persistent whine as those on the Hummers that had been chasing the horses on Thursday. When all the motors had been killed, he could hear the drivers jump from their vehicles and slam their doors. There seemed to be three people.

All three walked to a spot that was probably just in front of the truck. They began to whisper. Someone, a man, coughed and spit on the ground, and shortly after that, he heard heavy footsteps coming toward him. Soon the ropes that bound his hands and feet to the side of the trailer had been freed, and someone grabbed his left ankle and pulled him out of the trailer. He landed on his back with a heavy thump. For several seconds, he lost his breath. When he was breathing again, one of his captors pulled him up by the arm and shoved him roughly away from the trailer.

After he had stumbled along for several yards, the man shoved Ben into the needled branches of a ponderosa tree, then pushed him down alongside the trunk. He could feel the spikes from the lower bough picking at the hair on the top of his head. The man kneeled to wind a rope around Ben, pinning his arms down and anchoring him securely to the tree, then the man crawled backward and checked the tape on his feet. When he was sure Ben was immobilized, the man scooted out, and Ben could hear him climb back into the truck that pulled the trailer, start the motor, and pull away. Within a few minutes, the other two vehicles followed.

The sparse branches above him and the bag on his head were at least providing some protection from the storm. The rain was driving against the heavy plastic of the bag making a noise not unlike the sound it made when it splattered against his bedroom window. He tilted his head down to use the bag as an umbrella for as much of his body as possible. Good thing the wind was at his back.

In a few minutes, the rain retreated, and Ben raised up his head. He thought he heard voices. He sat perfectly still, taking care not to move the bag on his head, so it wouldn't make rasping sounds that would cloud his hearing.

Yes, someone was talking. It sounded like the voices were coming from some distance away. Whoever was speaking didn't seem to be moving, and the conversation was muffled, yet staccato, as if someone were talking from behind a heavy mask and trying to enunciate clearly, so another could hear.

Instantly, he knew what it was. There were others tied not far from him, and they too had these heavy plastic shrouds over their heads.

As soon as he was sure, he called out, "Hey, who's out there?"

Nothing, just silence. Ben's stomach rumbled in fear, but he tried again. "Hey, it's Ben West. I'm tied to a tree over here. Who are you?"

Still no answer.

He tried several more times, but no one shouted back, and although he listened intently, he heard no voices after that.

About twenty minutes later, Ben heard the motor of the truck. It sounded like it was driving above him, at the top of a rise behind him. Soon, he heard a door slam, and then a loud "crack" as someone shot a rifle. Ben could hear the bullet pass above him through the sparse branches of the tree. There was another, then another, all seemingly aimed at the tree to which he was tied. A slight pause, then three more shots, only this time the rifle seemed to be shooting toward a target about 20 yards to Ben's right. Another pause, then three more shots that seemed to be shooting toward something even further to the north.

When the sound of the rifle had died away, a man's loud voice broke through the misty air. "O.K., you guys, I'm comin' down. I'm gonna untie your hands and feet—and we're gonna let you go, but if you take the bags off your heads or look up before we're gone, this guy up here with rifle will shoot you dead."

Ben could hear the man's feet stumble against the rocks as he climbed down the slope of the bluff. He tramped past Ben and continued across the little valley, behind what Ben suspected was an irregular row of sturdy, but straggly ponderosas. He heard the man scuffling on the ground as he unwound the ropes from the other captives, then he came over to Ben, untied the knot, and crawled back and forth to unwind the rope and free him. He pulled him up and gave him a rough shove. Ben's legs were stiff, and he bumped against someone else who had been standing just opposite the tree to which Ben had been tethered. He could tell other person was also wearing a plastic bag and seemed to be just about his size. Somehow, it was encouraging to know that he wasn't the only one in this awful scrape.

The man took one of Ben's wrists and snipped the plastic ring that encircled it, and then Ben heard a snipping sound that told him he did the same to the others.

"Sit down and take off your shoes and socks," said the man. His voice was guttural. Ben thought he was trying to disguise it. Ben was tempted for half a second to ask if boots counted as shoes, but thought better of it, dropped to the ground and removed his footwear.

"O.K., now stand right there." The man put his hands on Ben's shoulders and placed him in a way that Ben thought was square in front of the bluff. He could hear him do the same with the others.

"Now, one piece at a time, throw your shoes—or boots—and socks as high and as far as you can. Don't try ta fake me. If you don't throw 'em far enough, I'll use one a these dead branches against the side a yer head."

First his socks, then his boots went into the air. Ben heard them plop some distance in front of and above him. He could hear the others' footgear land as well.

The man grunted an "O.K." in satisfaction and then said, "Now turn around and get down on your hands and knees." When they were on the ground, he directed, "Now crawl straight forward—and don't stop, no matter what—or my friend upstairs'll shoot you."

Ben began to crawl. He was ashamed that he wanted to cry. The bag over his head made it impossible to see anything, and there was something about being on his hands and knees that made him feel like he was completely defenseless. After they had crawled a few yards, he heard a shriek of pain from whoever was under the bag to his far left.

"Don't you dare stop—not if you wanna live," growled the man, and Ben thought he heard a soft thud—someone being kicked.

Another squeal and a whimper.

"Go on!" rasped the man. "This isn't gonna kill you."

Then the other person, a male voice immediately to his left, let out a screech of surprise and started to weep softly.

"I said keep crawlin'," said the man fiercely.

Ben's stomach was a dark knot of fear. He dreaded whatever it was that he was sure awaited him just beyond. He hit it just a few seconds later. When he put down his left hand, something stabbed it, and he instinctively snapped it back up. When he hesitated, not wanting to crawl forward, the man behind him put his foot on Ben's rear and shoved it forward. He was able to catch himself, so he didn't fall flat, but his hands were searing where they had been punctured. He knew now what the enemy was—a thick patch of prickly pear cactus. Blindly, he crawled forward, wondering how far they would have to go. His knees, shins, and the tops of his feet felt like they were on fire, and even the tops of his hands were burning with the pain of the needle-like stickers that grew in all sizes on this hardy little plant.

He remembered reading that the prickly pear was the enemy that almost defeated Louis and Clark as they made their way to the Pacific, the awful stickers invading the explorers' feet, the ear-shaped cactus so deadly in its abundance and resilience. The largest needles were big—three to four inches long—and tough; the Native-Americans used to use them for sewing. The smallest ones were hair-like, invisible to the naked eye. They slid under the skin and hid for months, finally working their way out through a pus-filled lump.

Ben crawled forward, thinking his captor must have been gathering the plants when he was circling around before he had tied Ben to the tree—and then he had scattered them in a path. The cactus plants rarely grew so close together or in such a predictable pattern. When he finally reached the end of them, the man directed him to stand up and walk back the way he had come. By then, the pain was at such a level that the new stickers on the bottoms of his feet barely made an impact.

At the end of the row of prickly pears, the man stopped him and removed the plastic rings that still dangled from one of his wrists. He could hear him doing the same with the others. He pushed all of them to the ground and scrambled up the rise.

"Don't take the bags off your heads until you can't hear the truck," yelled the man. "We have a sniper with a scope in the back of the trailer."

Ben heard the motor of the truck rumble up again, and he sat there, afraid, trying hard not to sob in frustration and pain.

They waited until the only sounds they could hear were the occasional shriek of a hawk and the friendly rustle of the breeze through the needles of the ponderosa. Ben took off his bag first. He looked at the other two figures seated pathetically on the ground beside him.

"It's O.K., they're gone," he croaked. He watched as the other two tore at the tape around their necks and lifted the bags off their heads. They looked at Ben, their eyes red, their faces blotched from anger and distress.

One of them said flatly, "Hi Ben."

Ben forgot his pain and stared in disbelief.

Chapter Fourteen

Misty sat in the truck, running the motor because she wanted to keep the windshield wipers going. The gas gauge showed over half full, so she wasn't worried. This pickup had a gas tank that held over 20 gallons. She hadn't turned on the lights, even though the afternoon had turned into almost-night. She thought she would see the lights from the ATV more easily if she kept the headlights on the truck turned off. Ben knew this part of the prairie so well, she wasn't concerned about his getting lost, but as soon as she saw the spots from the ATV, she would turn on the truck lights to better direct him to where she sat waiting for him. At one point, she thought she saw a pinpoint of light coming toward her in the distance, not far from the direction in which Ben had gone. It lasted for only a second, however, and she decided she had imagined it.

After Ben had been gone for over half an hour, the cell phone rang.

"Are you on your way home?" her father asked.

"Ben hasn't come back yet," Misty returned worriedly. "D'you think I should go look for 'im?"

"D'you know where he is?" asked her father.

"Not really," Misty said reluctantly. "He went over the hills to see where this light was coming from."

"Light?"

"There was a light to the north. I can't see it now."

"What kind of a light?" Hank's voice had an edge.

"Just kind of an goldish glow. Ben didn't think it was anything natural, wanted to see where it was comin' from," Misty said wearily.

"Well, he shouldn't have gone. If he had to see what it was, why didn't you kids just drive over there with the pickup?" asked her father.

"I don't know. I guess Ben thought it would be easier to get around the ravine on the four-wheeler— less likely to get stuck if the rain got worse," said Misty. "Do you think I should go look for 'im?"

There was a pause. Misty could hear her father talking to her mother, both of them concerned that Ben had gone off alone in an uncovered vehicle in a rainstorm.

"Any lightening out there?" asked Hank.

"Nope," said Misty. "It's starting to rain pretty hard, though."

"Exactly where are you?"

"I'm sittin' on the stem side of Apple Rock."

"Well, stay there. I'm gonna borrow one of John's trucks and come out there. If Ben comes back before I get there, you two stay where y'are now and wait for me," said Hank. He hung up the telephone.

Misty's stomach was starting to roll, and her eyes stung from staring into the murky dusk.

Twenty minutes later, she saw lights in her rearview mirror. She was relieved when she saw her father step out of John Lawford's old white pickup. He ran through the rain to where she was parked and motioned for her to hop over the gearshift, so he could get behind the steering wheel.

"Not here, huh?" said her father after he was settled into the driver's seat.

"Huh-uh." Misty shook her head and tried to blink away the tears that were crowding her eyes.

Her father snapped on the headlights and threw the truck into reverse, so he could take the shallower path down the hill.

"Tell me where to go," he said.

Misty coached him across the prairie where Ben had gone. Any tracks that had been made by the spirals that scored the big tires of the ATV were now entirely obscured by the downpour.

"Always happy to see any moisture, but I sure wish this rain wasn't comin' down just now," Hank mumbled as he concentrated on guiding the pickup around the wet sand of the unpredictable prairie dunes. After a fruitless half-hour of random travel in the direction in which Misty had last seen Ben, they began to zig-zag in deep, mile-wide patterns across the hills.

After twenty minutes, they found the red four-wheeler half on its side in the rut where its front wheel had been buried. Hank stood over it, wiping his nose on the wet sleeve of his jacket.

"Ben!" Misty shouted. "Ben! Are you around here?"

"He would have seen our lights," her father said quietly. He walked over to the pickup, extracted a flashlight from under the front seat, and began to walk a wide circle around the disabled ATV, looking for any sign of where Ben might have gone. About 50-feet out, he bent down to the ground and used the flashlight as a spot. He pointed it downward and walked a straight path of about 20 feet.

Misty walked over to see what he had found. She looked down to see that the prairie grasses had been pressed down by wide wheels, and that there were still vague grooves in the dirt below that showed the impact of the patterned rubber of heavy tires. There was nothing beyond, however. The terrain was gravel and sandstone. The rain had washed away any sign of where the vehicle had gone. Misty's father walked out for some distance, then returned and motioned for Misty to get into the pickup.

"Maybe we can pick up the tracks again," her father said as he picked up the cell phone. "Hi, Babe," he soon said to Misty's mother. "You hear from Ben?" Misty could hear her mother's worried denial.

"Well, we found the four-wheeler. He ran it into a ridge hollow. But we can't find Ben. Looks like maybe he started walkin' and someone picked him up. Probably somebody that was checkin' on the horses. You hang by the phone. Let me know if you hear from 'im." Silence as Misty's father listened to her mother, then "Well, I'll be damned. He call the sheriff?" More silence, then "No, they weren't Humvee tracks. Looked like a pick-up and a trailer. Probably Larry or somebody. We'll let you know what we find." Her father's confident voice didn't match the worried, furrowed expression that was on his face as he set the handset into its bagged cradle.

"Your mom just talked to Scooter, and he said he got hold of Jackie Campbell. She just returned from Australia, hasn't seen John Lawford since spring."

Hank shook his head and turned the pickup back the way they had come. "Damnedest few days I've ever been through," he muttered as he pushed the red truck over the rough roller coaster path back toward the place where the white truck was parked.

When they came in sight of Apple Rock, Hank said, "Since you were parked right under the stem side, it'd be pretty hard to see this truck. Maybe Ben was hurt, and whoever picked him up didn't know anyone else was around. They might have taken him to get some medical attention—might have gone the back way."

"I did see a flicker of light in that direction," said Misty, "but it lasted for just a second, and I thought maybe I'd imagined it. Then a few minutes after that, the light in the distance went out. It didn't go out all at once, it just sorted of faded out—but that could have been caused by the rain getting heavier."

The rain was passing. Only small, vaporous drops were falling now. The cold, late afternoon daylight was returning as blue sky made small patches behind the clouds. Her father took a wide swing to avoid a rut, and Misty rolled down her window, looking out, trying to see any sign of her brother. All she saw were rabbits—jacks and a few cottontails—celebrating their freedom in the now calm, still-drizzly afternoon. Then, to her surprise, she saw dark figures trailing from behind the bluff in the distance. Misty reached for the binoculars in the seat in back of her. When she had the objects in focus, she saw that it was the Arabians; the big liver chestnut with the red shoulder was at the head of a lop-sided line.

Misty held her breath, then breathed, "The Arabians are over there by the bluff. Mirage—er Mohit—is still there at the front."

Her father slowed the pickup to a stop, motioned for her to sit back, so he could look through her window, and took the glasses. "Looks like he's O.K.," he said. "That's one beautiful horse." He sighed. "If he's as smart as he is good-lookin', it's no wonder everybody wants 'im."

He scanned the area and started to hand the glasses back to Misty, then abruptly, with a scowl, he raised them to his eyes again. "Well, I'll be damned," he said softly. "Looks like there are some people on the ground over there to the left." He shifted the pickup into drive, made the turn and started toward the bluff.

Misty looked through the powerful binoculars. She could see three tiny figures on the ground, coming toward them by bouncing along on their backsides, using their elbows as leverage. They were about a football field to the left of the horses. She was surprised her father had spotted them at all against the dark shadows in the sandstone.

"One of 'em's Ben," Misty said as they drew closer. "Can't imagine who the other two are. They're bunglin' along like upside down snakes." In a few minutes, she added, "It is Ben—and if I didn't know better, I'd swear the other two are the Sandler boys. They're movin' slow as crippled turtles, and not one of 'em has any shoes or socks on."

Chapter Fifteen

Ten minutes later, Hank stopped the pickup on the near side of a dry creek bed, and he and Misty walked down to meet the three boys. Their hair was plastered to their heads, water was running down their faces, and their sweatshirts were hanging wet from the rain. They were moving jerkily as if they were on hot coals. After they slid down the hill and reached the soft sand at the edge of the creek bed, they all sat up and began to examine the soles of their feet. Hank and Misty skidded down the bank opposite to where they sat. Brett, the younger Sandler looked up with eyes that were red and swollen, his round face a theme of distress, and Misty could tell from the way Ben had his lips clenched together that he too was hurting and upset.

"You guys O.K.?" asked Hank.

They all nodded.

"What the hell's goin' on?" Hank kneeled down beside Ben.

"We ran into some bad trouble, and we're sure glad to see you two. I was afraid we'd have to crawl all the way back to Apple." Ben's voice broke.

"What's wrong with your feet?" Misty asked. The boys were holding their feet and picking at them, but she couldn't see any blood or bruises.

"They made us walk in the prickly pears before they let us go," said Ben. He was shivering and trying to pull invisible stickers from between his toes. "Even made us crawl in 'em."

"Ugh!" Misty groaned, thinking of the razor-sharp, hair-like stickers that protected the mitten-shaped prickly-pear cactus.

"Who are *they*?" asked her father.

"Don't know. Never saw their faces—never saw their trucks. They came up behind me after I spilled off the ATV. Put a bag over my head and someone hauled me in a trailer over to where they had these guys." He nodded his head at the two young men who were sitting awkwardly in the sand beside him, clasping their arms about their shoulders, their teeth chattering. "Neither one of them saw the guys or heard 'em talk either."

Hank stared at the Sandler brothers. One, Brady, the older one, the tall one, was heavy-boned but lean, with thick brown hair, a square open face, and an earring in one ear. The younger, Brett, was pear-shaped and soft with a bleached yellow crew cut. He was no taller than Misty. One of his bright blue eyes was lazy and wandered slightly toward his nose. Misty remembered that Brett had once worn a patch over one of his eyes.

"Aren't you two supposed to be in jail?" asked Hank uneasily.

"Well, sort of. They put us in the detention boot camp over by Ponderosa," said Brady as he ran his finger shakily over the stickers on the bottom of his big toe.

"Well, why aren't you there?"

"We went over the fence about a month ago. Mr. Lawford's been lettin' us camp here on his place since then. We been livin in that old pioneer cave about four

140

miles over there." Brady pointed to the bluffs in the distance. "He brings us food and stuff."

"How come we never heard you escaped?" asked Misty, thinking that now she knew why Mr. Lawford had so many boxes of snacks and other easy-to-prepare foods.

"They don't know we did," said Brady. "My ma made up some phony transfer papers and sent one of her cousins in an armored van to pick us up. They swallowed it all, and he dropped us off here."

"My ma even called the camp from her cell phone and pretended she was an administrator at the jail," said Brett, who couldn't resist a slight smile. "No pun intended—anyway she let 'em know we got to the new place. The detention camp thinks we're in Missouri somewhere."

"Why would Mr. Lawford hide you boys?" Hank tilted his head to one side and looked down at them skeptically.

"Number one, 'cause he knows we're innocent, and number two, 'cause he can't stand to see anything penned up." Brady continued to examine his feet, then carefully pulled the leg of his jeans above his knee. Delicately, he ran his finger up his shinbone and over his knee.

"I'm covered with these damned things," he said roughly.

"And how did you get caught out here—and who caught you?" asked Hank.

"Never saw who got us," said Brady. "Came in the middle of the night, put bags over our heads and used plastic cuff things on our hands and feet. Threw us in

141

a trailer, took us over backa that bluff and dumped us out under a tree, chained us up and gave us a gallon of water with a straw. Made a teeny hole in each of our bags below our mouths. Told us that if the hole was any bigger when they got back, they'd shoot us. We believed them. Then this afternoon they brought Ben and threw him beside us."

Ben picked up from there. "About half an hour after I got there, they fired some bullets into the tree above us. Scared us spitless. Then this guy yelled at us from the top of the bluff. Told us they were going to let us go, but not to take the bags off our heads or look up or they'd shoot us. Somebody came down, took the stuff off our wrists and ankles, and made us take our shoes and socks off and throw 'em up in the air toward the top of the bluff. Then he made us crawl over to a gravel patch where there was a bunch of prickly pears. Made us crawl through 'em, then walk right on top of 'em."

"Then." said Brett, "that guy hightailed it up the bluff. He took the tape and plastic things with them. He kept shouting at us not to take the bags off our heads until we couldn't hear the truck anymore, said there was a sniper on the back of the trailer. He was probably lyin'," "But we weren't gonna take any chances. We were all so scared, we were shakin' like shingles in a tornado."

"What did you do with the bags?" Hank asked.

Ben turned on his side and pointed at something black protruding from the seat of his pants. "We folded 'em inside out and stuck 'em in the back of our jeans. We could tell they were wearin' gloves, but we thought the bags might have somethin' on 'em that would help find those guys." Ben looked up at his father. "Dad, I could be wrong, but I think those Humvees were there too."

Hank nodded, and then he and Misty stood for several seconds, staring at the three boys. "Well, we need to get you out of here," Hank said finally. "Misty, get those canvas tarps out of the pickup."

They folded one of the tarps and positioned it against the cab at the back of the bed of the pickup. Then one by one, they had the boys settle themselves as comfortably as they could on the other tarp, and Misty and her father dragged them out of the creek bed, through the wet sand and between the yucca plants. Then they helped them slide onto the bed of the pickup. The boys sat carefully, leaning against the cab, side-by-side, with their legs and feet straight out before them. Ben was in the middle. Hank threw the other tarp over them to help keep them warm.

As Misty and Hank moved forward to get into the cab of the truck, a small smile crept past the pain on Brady's face. "Kind of a *sticky* situation, isn't it fellas?"

"Yeah, I get the *point*," said Brett, teeth chattering. He elbowed Ben in the side.

"That's *barb*arous thing to say." Brady's voice was just above a whisper.

"But at least we still have a *sliver* of our sense of humor," Ben said finally, his voice uneven as the truck moved over the rocks and up the hill.

Inside the cab, Hank was trying to telephone Angela on the bag phone, but he couldn't get dial tone.

143

All he got was a fast busy, indicating no signal. With a sigh, he put down the handset and turned the pickup in the direction of the marooned four-wheeler. When they found it, he and Misty jumped out and stood over it.

"What d'ya think?" Hank asked Misty. "I don't want to leave it here. The way things are goin', it might not be here when we come back lookin' for it."

"I think we can pull it out," said Misty.

"So do I," said Hank. "You get the chain."

Misty went back to the pickup and pulled out a heavy chain that was in a box under the driver's seat. She gave it to her father, and he hooked it around the trailer extensions at the back of both vehicles. Within minutes, the little red ATV sat primly on the side of the rut that had caused its upset. Hank swung his leg over to sit on the seat and turned the key; a rolling series of unperturbed put-put-puts bellowed from the little machine's engine.

"You drive the truck," Hank said to Misty. "I'll follow with this—has plenty of gas. Take it kind of slow, and keep me in your rear view mirror."

Misty drove with all her senses, trying to avoid rough spots and inclines, so her passengers in the back wouldn't be thrown about. She was also keeping an eye out for the horses, since they had seen them heading in this direction. She didn't see them, however, and after her father had loaded the ATV in the white pickup, they started toward Lawford's. She was relieved when she saw the big white house in the distance. Finally, they pulled up beside the front porch, and her father hauled up beside them seconds later.

"You go tell your mother what happened. I'll help the boys in."

Angela was coming out the front door as Misty climbed the steps. "Where have you been? Did you find Ben? Why didn't you call?" Her contralto voice was breathy with anxiety.

"Ben's O.K. He's in the back of the truck. The phone wouldn't give us dial tone—"

Angela whipped around her daughter and tripped down the steps. When she could see into the bed of the pickup, she stopped. Her face was contorted with confusion as she saw the three boys scooting on their backsides toward the open end-gate of the truck bed.

"Where in the world did you boys come from?" She glared at the Sandler brothers.

"It's a long story, Ma'am," Brady Sandler looked at her over his shoulder with a sad smile.

"They broke out," offered Ben as he thrust his feet over the extended end-gate.

"Shouldn't you call the sheriff?" Angela looked at Hank.

"I mean to," said Hank, "but first I'd like to hear what these boys have to say—and I don't think they're goin' anywhere in their present condition. Misty, see if you can find some tweezers."

Misty remembered there had been two Swiss army knives in one of the kitchen drawers when they had cleaned the day before. After she had picked them out from beneath some kitchen tools, she went into the bathroom and looked in the cabinet above the sink.

She found a set of tweezers. She brought them out as her mother was directing the boys to stretch out on chairs in the side porch where the light was best.

Her father and mother pulled out the tweezers that were part of the Swiss army knives. Misty used the pair she had found in the bathroom. She also produced two magnifying glasses she had taken from Mr. Lawford's bedroom—one from the nightstand and one from a bookshelf. They positioned reading lamps on the table above the boys' feet, and they began to extract the little stickers.

The Sandler boys had been going barefoot a good bit of the time they spent at the boot camp; consequently, the stickers weren't packed into the bottoms of their callused feet quite as abundantly as they were on the soles of Ben's softer feet. But Ben's legs were skinny and almost hairless, so he could see and feel the stickers there; whereas, the quills had buried themselves like brushes among the fuzzy hairs on the Sandler brothers' thick legs. Recovering them would be a miserable task.

"It'll be months before you boys get out all these stickers," said Angela. She looked at her husband. "Maybe we should take them into the hospital."

"They'll probably end up there or in a doctor's office, but until we decide what to do with 'em, we might as well get the stickers out of the balls of their feet—make it so they can walk on their tiptoes at least."

He pulled up a chair in front of Brady's feet. "Okay, Brady, I wanna hear why John Lawford would let two fugitives camp out at his place. I also wanna know why those guys today wanted you and Ben outa the way. I promise I'll give you a fair hearing. I'll tweeze and you talk."

Brady looked at his brother. His brother shrugged his shoulders as if to say, "What else can we do?"

"Well, first of all, I really have no idea what those guys today were after, but I do know that Brett and I have seen lights across the prairie, just like Ben did." He held his breath as Hank picked at his foot. "A coupla times, we hopped on the Arabians we'd been ridin' for Mr. Lawford and went across to where we had seen 'em. By the time we got there though, there was nothin' but fresh cow pies and tracks—from a truck and trailer and from somethin' else, that after talkin' to Ben musta been Hummers."

"Why were you riding Arabians for Mr. Lawford?" Hank asked as he held the magnifying glass over Brady's extended big toe.

"Well, we were kinda watchin' over his horses for him—especially when he was gone. He said these two mares were well broke, and they probably wouldn't be comin' into heat, that they'd be good for ridin' slow. Said that's what we had to do to pay him back for hidin' us out 'til my mom found a place for us."

"How'd you catch 'em?" asked Misty.

"Didn't have to. Those two never did go off with the rest of the herd—stayed close by in a little pasture Mr. Lawford had fenced off," Brady replied. "Those mares were pretty temperamental at first, one of 'em had an awful habit of chargin'. When we tried to catch her, she'd wait 'til we were real close, then she'd come at us full force with her teeth bared. Brett, he's pretty good with horses—had to get firm and catch her across the nose with a good stick a coupla times to break her of it."

"Hated to do that, but there just ain't any other way I know of to break a horse of chargin'," Brett added.

Hank nodded his head.

"The other one, she was just headshy," Brady went on. "She'd throw her head right up if Brett tried to bridle her. Kicked too. But since I was taller, she cooperated with me a little better, and we used a flicker fastened on with a rubber band to cure her of her kickin'." He paused. "Funny thing, though, even though at first those Arabians were skittish when we were catchin' em or tackin' 'em, they both have the lightest mouths Brett and I ever rode. When Mr. Lawford gave us those snaffle bits, we wondered if we'd be able to manage those high-strung mares with somethin' that light—that just nudges the corners of the horse's mouth. But once we were on top, it was like the horses knew what we wanted to do before we ever gave 'em the message."

"Mr Lawford would say that's cause they're Arabians," said Misty. "What do they look like?"

Brett answered. "The bigger one, the one Brady's been ridin' is a light chestnut, a beautiful reddish gold with a blond mane and tail and a copper strip runnin' down her back. I've been ridin' the bay—kind of a dark red with a black mane and tail and two white stockings. She has the black ears and black knees—and a faint star on her forehead—never saw a horse quite like her before. They're beautiful animals—'course all John's horses are beautiful. You'd think he'd get a ringer, lettin' 'em breed at will the way he does."

"That's what we've been sayin'," said Hank. "So go on Brady, why'd John let you come there in the first place?"

There was a long pause, and then Brady went on, "Well, John knew my dad." He looked up. "Mr. West, did you know my dad?"

"Jest by sight, never did talk to him much," said Hank. "I know he was a hell of a horse trainer at one time."

"Yeah, well, he's other things now," said Brady.

"You seen him lately?" asked Hank.

"Yeah, he came back about a year ago," said Brady softly.

"Why haven't we seen him?" Hank came back.

"Cause he didn't want you t'see him," Brett replied.

"He was livin' in one a those old empty trailers on the other side of the section behind our house, connected it up to the water pump and the gas line. The windows were all blocked up, so people couldn't see in," said Brady.

"Why didn't he want anybody to see him?" asked Angela.

"Cause he was doin' some deals he didn't want anybody to know about," Brady said softly.

"What kind of deals?" Hank asked.

"Well, one of 'em had to do with some horses— and one of 'em was makin' meth," Brett finally answered. He looked up at Hank with a glaze of tears in his eyes.

"*He* was makin' the meth? Did you help him?" asked Hank.

"I don't know—didn't mean to. We went into Cheyenne and bought some stuff for him at first, didn't know what it was for. When we found out what he was doin' with it, we quit." Brady shifted in his chair and stared, glassy-eyed at Angela. "We were pretty dumb about it, then after we knew what he was doin', we tried to get him to tear it down, to quit makin' it. We were afraid he'd do himself in. That potato cellar isn't very well vented, and we knew by then that those chemicals were really dangerous. The only thing we had nerve enough to do was destroy the stuff he was makin'. We used to go in when he was sleepin'—he usually worked at night, so he slept during the day—and we'd make it look like somethin' had busted or somethin' and get rid of most of what he was makin'. Then he got smart and started hidin' it, so we'd go over and try to find it, so we could get rid of it."

"You're lucky you weren't hurt by those chemicals," said Angela as she motioned for Brett to raise his foot up a little more.

"Yeah, well, that's why we weren't able to destroy as much as we wanted to—scared we'd get poisoned or burned or somethin'," Brett mumbled.

"Why didn't your mom stop him?" asked Misty.

"Cause she didn't know about it—until after we got caught," said Brady.

"Well, then why didn't she tell the Sheriff, so you guys didn't get put in jail?" asked Ben.

"Cause the people who were sellin' the stuff my dad made said they'd kill us all—my mom, my little brother, my dad, Brett, and me too—all of us. Said they'd do it in such a way that no one would ever guess it was murder," Brady said softly. "And we believed 'em, cause my dad believed 'em. If you'd a seen him when he told us about it—right after we got picked up. He was scared to death. Said he had to go somewhere and keep doin' what he was doin', or all our lives were worth nothin'."

"How did he get into such a mess?" asked Hank.

"I don't know, but my dad was always lookin' for a way to make a quick buck; that's one of the reasons my mom asked him to leave. He wanted to get enough money together to finance a spread like you've got— somewhere in Oklahoma or New Mexico—somewhere he could raise racehorses and kick back. Guess he started makin' meth before he realized how dangerous it was. Thought it was just a harmless high—*whatever that is*—that it brought in good money." Brady coughed and sniffed back tears. "He was sellin' it to these people who were sellin' it on the street—then he found out they were sellin' mostly to high school kids—and that it wasn't harmless at all. He tried to pull out, but it was too late." Brady paused, then he added, "He isn't a bad man."

"Then why did he let you go to jail? Why didn't he confess?" asked Angela with a twisted frown. Misty could tell her mother was uncomfortable with a story that made a parent the bad guy.

Brady answered tiredly, with no expression in his voice, "Cause the people who were sellin' it said they'd kill him before they'd let him talk to the police.

They're afraid. He knows too much. They wanta keep him away from the law."

"Did you ever see the people he was sellin' it to?" asked Hank.

Brady shook his head. "We watched too. Never did figure out how he was gettin' rid of it."

"Well, you and your mom have really put yourselves in a spot tryin' to protect him. You two are prison escapees, and she aided in your escape." Hank looked up at Brady with a serious and gloomy expression on his face.

"Yeah, I know," said Brett, "but the alternative was pretty bad. Word was that they were gonna kill Bret and me in the detention center, 'cause my dad's disappeared."

"Who told you they were going to kill you?" asked Hank.

"Got a telephone call one Sunday afternoon," said Brett. "Some woman who told the warden she was our aunt. Had a tinny voice and southern accent. Told us that our dad was missin'. Asked if Brady or I knew where he was. We said we had no idea. She said she was gonna call my mom on Friday, and if my mom didn't tell her where he was then, the whole family would probably go up in smoke—that they had ways of getting' into the camp to get us." Brett swallowed. "We believed her."

"My mom arranged the phony transfer for the next Thursday," said Brady matter-of-factly, "and then my mom and little brother went to hide out at her cousin's place."

"Did John Lawford know you weren't guilty?" Hank sat back and looked at Brady doubtfully.

"Not at first—not 'til my mom made this deal with him," said Brady.

"What deal?" asked Hank.

"Well, my mom needed money to pay for our attorney fees," said Brett finally. "I don't know the details, except that my dad had told her before he left that he knew somebody who wanted to do a deal with an Arabian horse. Said a good friend of his had been trainin' this fancy horse, that the owners were out of the country for a few months, and he was s'posed ta take him to reining school in Arizona somewhere. Told her t'see what John Lawford would do in exchange for a visit from an Arabian stallion with a bloody shoulder."

Hank's hand that held the tweezers stopped in midair and his mouth dropped open. Misty pushed Ben's foot aside and turned to stare at Brady Sandler. Angela pushed her chair back and crossed her arms over her stomach.

"And how much did he pay?" Hank finally asked.

"I'm not sure who paid or what they paid, but I know my mom got about $25,000 for brokerin' the deal," said Brady.

"And that was a pretty small part of what changed hands," added Brett.

"How do you know?" asked Hank.

"Cause my mom said she wondered what kind of a ranch the trainer was lookin' ta buy with what he was makin' on this deal. Said it must be in California or somewhere," said Brett.

153

"California ranch land is pretty expensive," said Brady.

Hank West stood up. "I think I'd better call the sheriff," he said.

Chapter Sixteen

"Thanks Mr. Nolde." Tony jumped out of the green pickup. He watched as it backed around to drive out of the yard, and Lono leaned out the window to wave back with a grin. Tony stood watching after her, wishing they were going out tonight. It would be so decent when he had his driver's license, so they could go on a real date—maybe not alone even, maybe with some of their gang—but without Misty or one of his parents playing chauffeur. He'd heard they were going to open the old drive-in theater in Kilpatrick. That'd be a kick—to have Lono next to him in the front seat— in the dark—just the two of them.

He turned back to the ATV they had unloaded from Lono's father's truck. He would put it away after he checked in the house to see if there were any messages. From the dark windows, it was obvious no one was home.

When he kicked his boots off in the hallway, he saw a note on the table beside the black wall telephone. It was from Claire: *Tony, your parents and all are still over at Lawford's. Said to STAY HOME!! They'll call before they leave there. Charlie and I are home if you want to come over there. There is some lasagna in the fridge for supper.* Tony picked up the telephone to dial his mother's cell. The dial tone was pulsing, indicating there was a message in the call notes box. He dialed the number of the message service, entered the password, and was surprised to hear Mr. Lawford's voice.

"Hank, Angela, I need your help. I've got myself inta somethin' that's way deeper than I thought. I know Scooter's been tryin' to get holda me, but I need to leave him outa this just now—might get *him* inta this mess too. I jest need for you to go over and get some papers for me. They're in..." The message ended. Tony hit "K" on the keypad to save the message, then listened to it again.

Tony felt goosebumps crawl up his arms. He pressed the switch hook on the telephone, then dialed his mother's cell phone. She answered on the second ring.

"This is Angela West."

"Hey, mom, it's me. I just picked up the strangest message from Mr. Lawford." Tony spoke rapidly, taking a deep breath at the end of the sentence. "He said he wanted you and dad to get some papers for him, then just before he said where they were, the message cut off. I saved the message."

There were a few moments of silence before Angela answered. "Oh, lord, what next?" she said finally. "Are you at home?"

"Yep," said Tony. "Did you guys ever find those papers we were looking for?"

"No, could be he was talking about the same papers," said Angela, "but I really have no idea what he needs."

"Well, it would seem the papers he's talking about are still on the ranch somewhere—or somewhere where you could find 'em," Tony said. "You can go into the saved messages and listen to it."

"All right," she let out a long sigh. "Scooter talked to the lady in New Mexico. She hasn't seen John since spring." Angela's voice was tight with concern. "And your brother and—uh, your brother was kind of kidnapped this afternoon." She wasn't ready to explain the presence of the Sandler brothers.

"Kidnapped?" Tony said doubtfully. "Whadya mean *kidnapped*?"

"He ran aground on the ATV, and some men blindfolded him, made him walk in some prickly pears, and let him go," said his mother. "He's pretty uncomfortable."

Tony raised his hand to cover the slight smile on his face as he imagined his nimble twin with prickly pear stickers in his feet. He recovered quickly after he remembered how painful and how stubborn those hair-like thorns could be. "Whoa, that's heavy," he said, "Any idea who it was?"

"Not the slightest, but we've called the Sheriff. He's on his way out here. It'll probably be a while before he gets here, though. He was taking some deadbeat dad to Kilpatrick to put him in jail." Angela sniffed, then said, "Here, talk to your dad."

"Tony?" His father said. "You O.K.?"

"Sounds like I'm a lot more O.K. than Ben," said Tony.

"Yeah, well listen, why don't you go over to Charlie and Claire's. I'd feel a lot better if you weren't alone. Weird things are happenin'," said Tony's father.

"That's the second time in two days you've told me that," growled Tony. "And I don't need to go over to

157

Cooper's. I'm just fine here by myself. Anyone comes around, I'll get out my '22."

"That's the last thing I want you to do—start messing with guns," said his father quickly, angrily.

"You know I'm careful," replied Tony.

"Don't you even *think* of unlockin' that gun cabinet. That'd be the first step toward gettin' shot," said Hank. "You jest git yourself over t'Cooper's house—and stay there until your mom and I get home."

"Don't you want me to feed the cattle?" asked Tony. "It's way past time."

"You get Charlie to help you if you do. I don't want you wanderin' anywhere alone."

"Can I talk to Ben?" Tony asked.

"Just a second," said his father, and he pushed the MUTE button on the telephone. "Don't mention the Sandler boys just yet. Let's see how this all plays out. The sheriff doesn't even know they're here."

Ben nodded, pushed the MUTE button, and then said, "Ho!"

"So you took a stroll in the prickly pears," said Tony.

"Yeah, it's worse than the time we got into the chiggers when we were makin' tents under the willows," groaned Ben.

"Who got hold of you?"

"Danged if I know." Ben went on to tell Tony how he was captured and how they let him go—without mentioning the Sandler brothers.

"Well, I'm goin' over to get Charlie to help me feed the cattle. I'll see you when you get home," said

Tony, then he carefully replaced the telephone handset in its cradle. He shook his head, pulled on his boots, and slammed out the back door, leaving the kitchen and hall lights burning.

The big yard light was on. Tony jogged across the yard, through the corral, around the stock truck, and up the gravel drive to knock on the Cooper's door. Their dog Moose, a frisky border terrier, yapped a staccato greeting from inside the house. Claire opened the door. "C'mon in Tony. I'm glad you're home. I just talked to your mom. Can't imagine what's happenin' around here."

Claire was a medium-size woman with a straight body and a large bosom. Her short reddish-gray hair was permed into the short, tight, woolly style favored by many women who lived on the wind-swept plains. She usually wore T-shirts or sweatshirts with some sort of painted, embroidered, printed, or quilted decoration on the front. Today she wore a sweatshirt Tony didn't recall seeing before—a black crew neck with autumn leaves scattered randomly across her rounded bosom and down one shoulder. It was pulled over black stretch pants.

The little dog beside her was no more than 10-inches from the ground, and with his reddish coat under a shaggy black overgrowth, seemed to almost match Claire in color. His short tail was wagging briskly and his small, v-shaped ears were cocked as Tony leaned down to pick him up.

As he began to scratch the happy little dog behind his ears, Claire reached up to give Tony a motherly pat on the back. "You and Lono didn't find anything with the ATV's though, huh?"

"Nope," said Tony. He turned to Charlie Cooper who was padding shoeless into the living room from the kitchen. "Dad said we should go together to feed the cattle."

"That's probably best," nodded Charlie. Charlie was about three inches taller than his wife, just under six-feet, and he was wide and flat-chested. Since his grandmother was a full-blooded Lakota Sioux, his skin was a light bronze, and his face was smooth. He wore plaid shirts, jeans, and cowboy boots year-round. In the summer, the shirts sometimes had short sleeves. If he went to a wedding or a funeral, he wore a fancier shirt and new, maybe even black, jeans with his best boots, but other than that his costume never varied.

He stood in his white socks beside his favorite black leather recliner, and he still had a paper napkin in his hand. "We're eatin' supper though. You had anything t'eat?"

"No," said Tony, leaning his head back, so Moose couldn't lick him in the face.

"Well, come on then," said Claire. She took Moose from his arms, and Tony left his boots on the tiled entry—a ritual everyone observed when they came into the Cooper's house. The soft brown wavy carpet in the Cooper's living room was very likely just as clean as when the carpetlayers from Kilpatrick had tacked it down five years ago.

"Don't sound like Ben'll be wearin' any boots for a while," said Claire as she put Moose back on the floor.

She walked across the room to get the little dog a treat from a dish that was on top of the big-screen TV.

"Well, there's worse things than prickly pears," she said resolutely. As Tony followed her into the kitchen, he saw that her sweatshirt had a slogan painted on the back. It said *Leaf me alone!*

Tony grinned. If there was anyone in the world who wouldn't survive being left alone, it was Claire Cooper. She thrived on company and got past the isolation of living 20 miles from the nearest town by belonging to three card clubs and tracking everything that went on at the Methodist Church in Littletown. She spent a good amount of time chatting with friends and relatives on the telephone and e-mailing them on the computer. She drew out the life histories from all the hired hands that came to work on the Diamond W, and she extracted every detail about any school or rodeo event the West children were involved in. She also took off with Charlie whenever possible for trips on the big Kawasaki motorcycles they kept in the back of their oversize garage. They had friends all over the country. Tony knew Claire gathered energy from being with people.

After four freshly assembled tacos, three brownies, and a big glass of milk, Tony was ready to do chores. He and Charlie pulled on their coats and gloves and started for the corrals where the horses and feeder cattle were waiting for their evening meal.

"I'll take the cattle. You tend to the horses," said Charlie.

"Sure thing," said Tony, and he started toward the horse corral that stretched down the side and around the back of the horse barn. A strong split-chestnut, post-and-rail fence that was a little less than six feet high ran around the outside. There were five horses in an area that was about the size of a football field. All the other horses the Wests owned were still out to pasture. Zelda and his father's big Irish draft horse were standing with their heads over the split rails, waiting for him to bring their oats and hay. Cadaver, Tony's black Thoroughbred and Charlie's Quarter Horse were walking slowly toward the front of the corral as they saw Tony coming to the barn. He turned on the light and grabbed a hay pincher, and then he walked to the back and used it to grab an oversize bale of hay. He dragged the bale out the side door of the barn to where the horses were waiting. Carefully, he divided it five ways, then he threw one down in front of each of the eager horses. He went back in then, to get the oats. He always gave them the hay first, because sometimes the greedy horses gulped down their grain too fast if you gave it to them up front. The hay took the edge off their appetites, and they chewed their food a bit better.

He was coming out of the barn when he heard the put-put of the ATV. Charlie was riding the machine Tony had left in the yard, and he pulled up a few feet from Tony and shouted over the noise of the engine.

"Get the brown pick-up and meet me in the machine shed." He pulled away before Tony could ask him any questions.

In a few minutes, Charlie was climbing into the pick-up. "Go out back to the other side of the stock chute."

"Why?" Tony asked as he backed the truck around to head in that direction.

"I wanna see if you see what I see," Charlie growled.

Tony drove to the back of the corral. As they crested the hill where the cattle chute rested, he knew what Charlie had seen. In the distance, there were yellow lights, glowing against the sky like those of a farmstead. Tony was sure that no settlement had sprung up in the last 24 hours, but he had no idea what it could be.

"What do we do?" asked Tony.

"Damned if I know," said Charlie. "Don't have any desire to take a roll in the prickly pears."

"Well, we should call the sheriff," said Tony.

"Already did that," Charlie tapped the cell phone in his pocket. "He's on the other side of Kneeley. It'd take him at least an hour to get here. Deputy Will is on his way to Lawford's, so he can't bring the 'copter. Besides, the sheriff and I sort of figured out that by the time he got here, the lights would be gone—judging by what happened earlier this afternoon."

Tony and Charlie turned off the truck lights, slumped down in the pickup and stared at the warm glow in the sky. After a few minutes, they saw the light grow stronger, then suddenly it was gone. They sat for a few more minutes, watching the sky, waiting for the lights to reappear.

Charlie pulled the phone from his pocket and dialed. After Claire answered, he said, "Me'n Tony are gonna take a ride out t'check on the cows in the north pasture. We'll be back in a hour or so." He listened for a few seconds. "Yeah, we'll be careful." He snapped the small phone into itself and put it back in his shirt pocket.

"D'you wanna drive?" asked Tony.

"Nah, just take it slow," Charlie replied, "and leave off the lights. Let's try drivin' by moonlight."

They started toward the hills where they had seen the glow in the sky. The three-quarter moon provided a half-light that created an ashen, but clear picture of the prairie terrain. They bounced along at a good pace. Charlie kept his eye dead on the spot where they were heading and gave Tony direction from time to time.

"Should be just over that rise," Charlie said after about 20 minutes.

"It didn't seem like it was this far away," said Tony.

"Yeah, I know—but I've chased enough prairie fires to know that when yer chasin' light in the dark, ya figure how far away it seems to be then triple it." Charlie still looked straight ahead.

"Why don't ya just circle around here fer a bit," Charlie said about five minutes later. Tony drove the truck in wider and wider circles over and under the hills. In a few minutes, Charlie pointed to a large area off to their left where the grass had been flattened. When they reached it, they could see tracks leading to the northeast. Tony stopped. Charlie grabbed a foot-long flashlight from behind his seat and jumped from the pickup. Tony followed. There were tracks all around—wide tracks from heavy vehicles—and there were fresh cow pies and indentations. For a few feet, Charlie followed the tracks that led out of the trampled grass to the north, then he came back and pushed back his hat.

"Looks like they're gone," he said needlessly and shined the light around the area, careful to keep the head of the beam close to the ground. He stopped and aimed at something under the leaf of a yucca plant, then took his gloves from his back pocket, put them on, and walked over to stoop to pick it up. Tony went over to see what it was. It was an empty box about the size of a ten-pack of AAA batteries. It was made from light cardboard bonded with rich gold foil.

"What the hell would they be doin' with this?" Charlie asked.

Tony went over to look. The label read *Youthlook, For Women Who Don't Want to Live with Hair Loss.* They stared at the box as Charlie turned it over in his hand.

"Maybe it's some animal rights outfit, tryin' to raise the self-esteem of steers with thinning hair," cracked Tony.

Charlie grunted a slight chuckle.

Tony pointed to something else that was fluttering among the flattened grass at their feet. He stepped over to pick it up, then remembered to slip on a glove before he took it in his hand. It was an empty white packet about half the size of a post-it note—glossy on the outside, lined with foil on the inside. There was no writing on it except for the number "9" stamped in the corner on one side. When he squeezed it open and turned it over, bits of yellow powder sprinkled onto his glove. Tony sighed. Now he would have to tell to his father about the yellow powder on his thumb the night he found the Dutch Belted calf.

Charlie flicked the packet back and forth as it rested on Tony's glove. They could tell it would fit perfectly into the little gold box. Tony went back to the truck and brought two zip-lock bags from a box they kept in the truck to encase test tubes when they took blood samples from livestock. They put the box in one bag and the packet in the other and put them in the truck. They stayed for another 10 minutes, methodically searching with the wide beam of the flashlight in front of them, but they found nothing more.

"Think we should follow 'em?" asked Tony hopefully as he walked with Charlie to the truck.

"Nope," Charlie said as he opened the door to the driver's side of the pickup. "I'm gonna get you home, so you can send an e-mail alert to all the ranchers you have addresses for. And while you're doin' that, I'm goin' ta start callin'—your folks, the sheriff—and we're gonna alert every livin' soul in four counties. I don't know what's goin' on, but this whole thing is really startin' ta irritate me."

Chapter Seventeen

The kitchen clock said ten minutes to nine when Deputy Will walked up the steps and crossed the front porch of the Lawford's big ranch house. When Misty opened the door, he took off his Rockies baseball cap and nodded a greeting.

"Sheriff told me to pick up the Sandler boys," he said flatly.

"They're on the dining porch," said Misty as she held the door open, so he could pass. She followed him through the hall and to the kitchen, staring at the black gun and the handcuffs dangling from the heavy leather belt that hung to one side over his faded blue jeans. So much for the uniform. He greeted her parents who were in the kitchen. Angela was pouring a cup of tea, and Hank was sitting on a stool with a telephone to his ear. Hank nodded his head sideways toward the room adjacent.

When Deputy Will reached the doorway, he stood with his hands on his hips, staring at Brett and Brady.

"Thought you two had a long reservation at the Ponderosa State Resort for Wayward boys," he said.

"We didn't like the food," said Brett.

Deputy Will didn't smile. Slowly, he shook his head. "Well, you got yourselves into a heap a trouble by decidin' to seek other accommodations."

"We woulda been in more trouble if we'd a stayed," said Brady.

"So I hear," replied Deputy Will. "Sheriff says I gotta take you two clear over to Southbluff to the doctor, then bring you back to Littleville and put you in our little one-room jail—doesn't want any publicity—in case your story checks out—and someone really is after you.

The boys nodded.

"You gonna give me any trouble?" The boys shook their heads. "Well, I won't put the cuffs on til we get in the car then." Ben watched, thinking something like this was much sadder when it was really happening than it seemed when you watched on TV.

"Hank told the sheriff they fixed it so you can walk," said Deputy Will.

"Just on our tip-toes," said Brett.

"Well now, this might be the first time I've ever had guys tippy-toeing into my cruiser," said Deputy Will with a lopsided smile. "Let's go." He motioned with his head toward the back door. "I'll bring the car around back here and pick you up." He looked around. "Where are your shoes?"

"Somewhere out on the prairie where the guys who did this to us threw 'em," said Brady as he braced his arms on the table and brought his weight onto the balls of his feet.

"Well, you can tell me all about it while we drive to Southbluff." Deputy Will turned to go through the house to get his car. He nodded at Hank, Misty and Angela, who were standing in the kitchen.

"We gave them something to eat," said Angela.

"Thanks," said Deputy Will. He started to go down the hall, then looked back at the three of them standing in a row in front of the counter. "Don't worry, I won't let nothin' happen to 'em." He turned to go out the door.

The telephone in Hank's hand rang as they watched Deputy Will's tail lights start down the long drive toward the front gate. It was Scooter, returning their call.

"Tony picked up another message from your dad," said Hank. "Sounds like he's pretty worried. Wanted us to go somewhere to get some papers. Didn't want you involved. He got cut off—or hung up—before he got to tell us everything he wanted to."

He listened for a long time, then said "No kidding! Well, from what we heard just a little while ago, I'm not surprised...," He talked for several minutes, describing what had happened that afternoon, then he listened again. "Yeah, that sounds like a good idea— might clear up a few things. I need to go. I've got another call. Call us when you know what you're gonna do."

When Hank tapped the switch hook of the telephone, it was Tony, phoning from the pickup as he and Charlie made their way home. Hank listened in disbelief as Tony related what they had found. After he said good-bye, he looked at Misty and her mother.

"Let's all go in there." He nodded toward the dining porch where Ben was stretched out, still picking stickers from his legs.

"Think you need to go to the doctor?" asked Hank as he pulled out chairs, so the women could sit down.

"I don't think so. I'm makin' pretty good progress." Ben was bent over his knees with the magnifying glass and the tweezers.

Hank sat and rested his folded hands on the table. "Scooter said he got hold of the woman who runs the horse farm where he first saw Mohit. She said the horse had been sent to reining school at a place outside Flagstaff, AZ. Says his trainer took him there in late September. S'posed to be there for a couple a years." Hank took a big blue handkerchief from his back pocket, swiped his nose, and sniffed. "He called the farm in Flagstaff, and they said Mohit's there—at pasture, restin' for the month, gettin' him acclimated before the training begins in November. I told him about the mares the Sandler boys have been watchin'. He says one of 'em sounds like the brood mare his father had sent him pictures of—the one he got in Kentucky. That makes sense. Anyway, Scooter says he's gonna ask a friend of his who has a plane to fly him to Arizona. Wants to look at the horse and talk to the people at the horse farm."

"Wow—I," said Misty.

"And what was Tony's story?" Angela interrupted.

Hank chewed the side of his lip for a moment and looked sideways at Misty. "Well, it seems he and Charlie saw some lights…"

Angela sat forward and grabbed Hank's arm. "Are they all right?"

"They're fine," said Hank emphatically. "They saw some lights in the distance when they were feedin' cattle, and they went up there after the lights went out. Found the spot, but there was nothin' there but an empty box and some kind of packet with a little yellow powder left in it."

Ben looked up at his father. "What kind of yellow powder?"

"Don't know. Tony said the package didn't have a label. Neither he nor Charlie had any idea what it was."

"What was in the box?" asked Misty.

"Well, they kind of think the packages might have come from the box. Said it was some kind of stuff for women to use to cover bald spots," said Hank.

"Did Tony or Charlie have any idea why it was there?" asked Angela.

"Not a clue," said Hank, "although Charlie was wonderin' if they weren't usin' it to cover somethin' up on the steers that have come up missin'."

"Like brands," said Misty.

"Could be," said Hank, "Anyway, Charlie and Tony are sendin' e-mails and callin' all the ranchers to put them on alert, and the sheriff's comin' out to our place in the morning. Tony said whoever was there left good tracks. Maybe the law'll be able to figure out where these guys are goin' or where they've been."

Angela looked at Ben. "I want to go home, Hank."

Hank took her hand. "So do I, babe." he said. "Ben, you think you can travel?"

"Sure," he nodded.

"But if all the ranchers are on alert, who's gonna be watching over this place?" asked Misty. "Shouldn't somebody be out in the pastures here, making sure that nothing happens to Mirage—er Mohit—and the other horses?"

"Well, they seem more interested in cattle right now," said Hank.

"But when we first saw them, they were around the horses," said Misty. "Maybe me 'n Tony could come back, just to let them know someone's..." She stopped abruptly when she saw the expression on her mother's face.

"Your mom and I feel our place is at the Diamond W, and I don't want you or Tony wanderin' around in the dark, like bait." Hank stood and pushed his chair under the table then leaned on the back. "C'mon, turn on a radio or something, so if anybody comes around, they might possibly think somebody's home, then...I'll tell you what—you and I'll take the plane. We'll circle around a couple of times to make sure no one's left on our place, and make sure no one's runnin' around John's pastures. See if we see any lights. That be O.K.?"

Misty nodded.

"Your mom and Ben can go home in the truck."

Hooter was parked in the level pasture south of the house. Within 20 minutes, Misty and her father were in the air. They circled around behind Apple Rock and over Picnic, but didn't see the horses—nor did they see any lights. Misty's father turned the little Piper Cub to the east where the Sandler brothers had said the two mares were pasturing. In a few minutes, they could see the stout fence that Brady had described. The horses were standing about ten feet apart on the far side of the enclosure, and they turned warily to watch the plane go over. It was hard to tell their color in the shadowy moonlight, but Misty could tell they both had high tails and widely flared nostrils—Arabian characteristics shared by all Mr. Lawford's horses.

As they eased the plane over the hills behind the mares, Hank made a wide circle to the northwest. Around a windmill and horse tank at the far end of a line of cottonwoods, no more than six or seven miles from the Diamond W, Misty spotted the herd of Arabians. Their dark shapes made a strange pattern in the murky light of the moon.

"I wish we could get closer without frightening them," said Misty, "close enough to make sure Mirage, or Mohit, or whatever his name is, is still there."

"Well, at least we know where they are, and we know that no one is after them—right now, at any rate," said Misty's father. "Let's go see if anybody's on our place." He pushed the throttle and maneuvered the plane to the left—to the west—toward the Diamond W.

Misty and her father spent an hour and a half circling over their pastures, but saw nothing unusual. When they finally parked Hooter in her hanger and drove the old gray Range Rover toward the house, they saw the truck parked at the Coopers and found Angela, Ben, Tony, and the Coopers gathered around the kitchen table. Pouring themselves a cup of hot cider, they joined them. They all sat, arranging and rearranging all the events that had occurred in the past two days, trying to make sense of it all—trying to create a picture of what the trespassers were doing and where they might go next.

"The thing I really don't understand," Misty said, "is the Humvee thing. If Ben and I hadn't seen them, we probably wouldn't have a clue about what made those wide tire tracks—the ones that weren't from the truck I mean—but why would they use Hummers? They aren't particularly fast, and they stick out like a sore thumb."

"Yeah, why not just truck in some horses and chase the cattle down with those?" said Ben.

"Well, you wouldn't have to feed and water a Humvee, and they would require a lot less care if you're travelin' a ways," said Charlie, "and they could definitely go 'bout anywhere horses or cattle could go. Did you kids get any kind of a look at those guys you saw drivin' 'em?"

"Not really," Misty answered. "They were pretty far away, and they had hats with wide bills that were pulled down, fatigue hats I think you call 'em, so we really couldn't see their faces very well. I couldn't even tell you what color hair they had, could you Ben?"

"Not for sure. They were definitely white guys though." Ben brushed his fingers over his knees, trying to find any remaining stickers. He raised his head. "There is one thing—I don't know if it's important or not, but when I was groomin' Zelda after our ride over to Lawford's on Thursday, I noticed some yellow powder on her back foot, on the inside of her hoof. It didn't smell or anything, but it definitely wasn't dirt—looked a whole lot like what's on the inside of that bag." He nodded toward the clear zipper bag with the packet in it that was lying on the table.

"I saw something that looks like that stuff too," said Tony. "When I wiggled that dead oreo calf's leg to see how long he'd been dead, I got some of that yellow powder on my thumb and under my thumbnail.

I'll bet if we looked at the dead calf again, we'd find some more."

Hank shook his head. "I can't believe you touched that dead calf without protection. What if he had anthrax or something?" He looked at Tony.

"Never saw anthrax break a cow's neck and leg," said Tony, "but yeah, I knew right away it was a dumb thing to do."

"Well, we'll give this stuff to the sheriff in the morning. He can send it away and have it analyzed," said his father, "and we'll go out to see if we're missin' any cattle."

It was after midnight when the Wests trekked across the yard to their house. Tony looked at the lights he had left on in the house, thinking that when he left, he had planned to be back a long time before now. He had stayed at the Cooper's after they returned from their trip to the north pasture, and he had used the their computer to send messages to all the ranchers, gathering the addresses from an e-mail he had sent to Charlie the day before about their new vigilante system. After everything that had happened that day, he was glad he had his family around him as he mounted the steps that led to the back entry. Once they were inside, his father went around to check the house, and everyone else climbed the stairs to their bedrooms.

Angela paused with Ben at the door to his room. "You going to be O.K.? Do you want an aspirin or something?"

"No, I think I got most of 'em out. I think I'll sleep fine." He turned to go into his room.

175

Once in bed, Misty slept in odd-hour spurts. She kept thinking of the horses, out in that pasture under the flat-sided moon, defenseless against the grating machines and their mysterious drivers.

Chapter Eighteen

Sunday morning. When the first light seeped across the sky at just before five, Misty was awake. She had the night jitters. The Arabians, led by the stallion with the bloody shoulder, had taken over her dreams and pulled her out of sleep. At 5:00 she flipped out of her bed and tiptoed next door to Tony's room. She rapped softly on the door and peeked in. Tony was reading, sitting up in his wagon-wheel bed, a leftover from the bedroom furniture his parents had purchased when the twins left their cribs. Ben's matching bed had been carried out of the house in pieces the summer before they were ten, after the boys had broken the headboard by making a hammock. They had tied ropes from the spokes in the headboard, then over the bedroom door and angled a bed sheet in between. It had held until both boys and two of their friends challenged each other for residence, and the spokes on the wagon-wheel headboard broke through before the solid oak door gave up its hinges.

Misty opened the still squeaky door a bit further and said softly, "You awake too?"

"Yeah," Tony grunted.

"I can't sleep. Thinkin' I might as well go do the chores. Wanna go with me?"

Tony was silent for a moment and his green eyes squinted at her. "Were you thinkin' of saddlin' up the horses and ridin' 'em out to the near pasture—just to make sure the cattle there have water and all?"

Misty grinned and nodded her head.

Tony pursed his lips, pushed down his covers, and kicked his feet out. "Well, we'd better get goin'."

Five minutes later, after hurriedly writing a note on the chalkboard to tell their parents they couldn't sleep and were starting the chores, they gently opened the back door and started for the barn under the hazy gaze of the yard light.

"Do you think we can get there and back before the folks wake up?" asked Tony.

"Well, probably not before Dad's up, so we'd better feed the cattle first."

They had the horses saddled in record time. Feeding hay to the cattle in the far corral usually took twenty minutes, but this morning they were finished in ten, even though they were working in the dark. As soon as the last forkful went over the fence, they jumped on their waiting horses, Misty on the faithful Cadaver, and Tony on his sleek black Thoroughbred, Jasper.

All three West children had been allowed to choose horses on their fourteenth birthdays. Misty had chosen a blue roan Tennessee walker that was now being trained for show. Ben found Zelda, his tough little Appaloosa, on the internet; she came from a horse farm in Colorado. Tony had picked his horse from a herd on Hendren's ranch.

Billy Hendren's dad, Carl, had raised racehorses for years, and this one, though from a line of winners, was a bit more headstrong than his owner wanted to deal with. Jasper was 16 ½ hands high, spunky, intelligent, and stubbornly independent. Tony loved the challenge. When Jasper came to the Diamond W, he was fully-grown, barely trained to the saddle and had a chip on his shoulder. He was Tony's horse for over six months before the horse allowed his new owner to sit on his back. Now the horse followed him like a puppy. Tony could walk anywhere and leave the horse's reins hanging loose. The Thoroughbred was never more than five feet behind him. If Tony stopped, the horse would edge up to where Tony could touch him. When Tony resumed his pace, the horse was with him. Even Lono, who was considered to be one of the best horsewomen in the Sandhills, couldn't get Jasper to go anywhere but where Jasper wanted to go. But for Tony, the horse would obey the slightest and most subtle command.

One evening in the summer Charlie Cooper had snapped a picture of the magnificent, raven-black horse with Tony on his back, running in silhouette against a brilliant pink sunset, the horse's blue-black mane and tail fanning out as he made a breeze. The photograph had won first prize in a photo contest run by *The American Horseman* magazine. Angela had a framed enlargement on the wall in her office.

In the Sunday morning dawn, Jasper and Cadaver galloped side-by-side toward the east fence along the ravine that ran for miles across both the Diamond W and the Lawford's place. Tony kept his horse to a steady gait, and he could hear the soft sneezing sound the horse made as he galloped. Mr. Hendren called it "high blowing" and said you often get it from high-spirited, well-bred horses when they are running. Some folks, amateurs, might think the horse wasn't

179

sound of wind. With this horse, it meant just the opposite. Tony knew the big Thoroughbred could cover the five or so miles to the edge of their pasture in half the time the raw-boned buckskin could run it, but he wanted to stay with his sister.

When they reached the gate to the six-foot fence that lined the border between Lawford's ranch and theirs, Tony leaned down with his head level with his stirrup and pulled the latch. They rode through, and then he used his foot to put the latch-pin back in place. From there, they rode steadily until they reached the place where Misty and her father had seen the horses the night before. The horses were gone, but the sand was scalloped with hoof marks, and the prairie grasses had been grazed down in spots.

"Let's try over that hill," said Tony.

They trotted off to the east, clearing the rise just as the sun became a blinding red ball on the horizon. As they averted their eyes, they could see horses scattered all across the valley to the south.

"Looks like the whole tribe is here," said Tony as he took the German binoculars from his saddlebag.

"Yeah, I don't think I've ever seen this many at once. They're not always together like this. Even that day the Humvees were chasing them, I could see a good part of the herd clear on the other side of the ravine."

Tony raised the glasses to his eyes. He scanned the horses carefully, from one side of the herd and back again. "I don't see him," he said.

"Let me see," said Misty, and she reached over to take the binoculars from Tony's outstretched hand.

"There he is," she said finally. "He's standing behind that group of little gray mares on the left side. I see Shadow too—over on the right side—with that beautiful chestnut with the odd markings. Remember her? She's the one Mr. Lawford used to ride sometimes. Has a star, strip, and snip that runs down into her left nostril." Misty handed the glasses back to Tony.

"I see him now," said Tony after a while. "And I see Shadow too and the chestnut too. I just wish we dared to get closer."

"I think they'd just get spooked. Their bein' all together tells me they may have been spooked already."

"How far away are those two mares the Sandler boys were riding?" asked Tony.

"Over about three sections that way," Misty nodded to the southeast.

"Think we have time to go over and look at 'em?"

"Nope, I think we'd better get home before we're grounded for life," said Misty.

Back at the Diamond W, they tied their mounts to the split rail fence that enclosed the back lawn of their house and went in the back door. Their father and mother were sitting stiffly at the old white metal table in the kitchen, half-rocking back and forth in the platform chairs made with chrome-plated tubing that had come through the back door in the 40's. Their parents were dressed in blue jeans and sweatshirts and weren't smiling. In fact, Misty could tell that her

181

mother had been crying. She braced herself for what was coming.

"Never knew you two to be so eager to do chores before," said their father.

Tony and Misty stood with their backs against the counter. Neither spoke.

Hank watched them with his eyes squinted. "So, was he there?"

Misty nodded.

"You sure?"

She nodded again. "He looked fine."

"Charlie and I were goin' out to check to see if there were any missin' calves and saw you two leave. Followed you with the pickup, kept you in sight til we saw you headin' for home. What the hell were you two thinkin' of, after what happened to Ben and all?" Hank's voice was soft, serious.

"I couldn't sleep all night. I just had to see if that horse was all right." Misty's eyes started to fill with tears.

Both Hank and Angela turned their eyes toward Tony.

"I couldn't sleep either, thinkin' that someone might be bothering Mr. Lawford's Arabians," said Tony. "I figured if we went up there the back way on horses, if there was anybody there, we'd see them a long time before they could see us, and we could get back home pretty easily through the ravine." Tony took a telephone out of his jacket pocket and laid it on the table. "Mom's cell was layin' here on the table; I grabbed it before we went out the door, just in case…"

Angela rose from her chair to walk across the kitchen to get a tissue from a box on the counter. She wiped at her nose, and then as she walked back to her chair, a long rat-a-tat ring came from the old black telephone on the kitchen wall. She stepped to the side to answer it.

"Oh, hi Scooter." She listened for a time, then said, "That's unbelievable, but they say it's Mohit?" She turned to the others. "Scooter says the horse at the farm in Flagstaff isn't Mohit—that it's a much more ordinary stallion that looks something like Mohit." She turned back to Scooter. "What about the bloody shoulder?" She listened and shook her head. "Well, we know Mohit is still with the herd. Misty and Tony just got back from riding horses over the back way to check. We're just now giving them the what-for for riding over there." She paused to listen. "That's what Tony said, but they still shouldn't have gone." She listened again. "O.K., I'll tell the sheriff, and we'll see you soon." She hung up the telephone and walked back to her chair shaking her head.

"He thinks they've used some sort of hair dye to make it look like the horse has reddish hair on his withers. It's a little lighter than Scooter remembers it." She thought for a moment. "Dying it wouldn't be too difficult, actually, if horse hair acts anything like human hair; my cousin's a brunette, and her hair always turned red when she tried to dye it a lighter color."

"From what we've heard in the last 12 hours, sounds like a guy could make a living if he opened an animal beauty salon," Hank snorted. "So is he comin' back here?"

"Yes, his pilot friend is flying him home, but he wasn't sure when they'd get here," said Angela. "He said he didn't tell the people at the horse farm they had the wrong animal—just oohed and aaahed over the impersonator—gave them the pilot's name instead of his own. Didn't want anybody to know he was snooping around. The man who showed him the horse told him the trainer who brought him wasn't there; he was on vacation or something. Said the trainer would be back sometime next week."

"Whoa, the plot thickens," said Ben from the doorway. He was wearing a red and white striped nightshirt he'd received for Christmas the year before.

"Hi, honey," said Angela, "How ya feelin'?"

"Well, I have a whole lot of little red spots on my legs where the stickers were and some still are, but it's better than last night." Ben started to walk gingerly toward the refrigerator.

"Oh, for heaven's sake, sit down," said Misty. "I'll get you whatever you want."

"Well, some fresh-squeezed orange juice sure would be nice—in a frosted glass—with maybe a slice of pineapple and a dollop of whipped cream." He turned awkwardly and dropped into an oversized, upholstered rocker that sat in the opposite corner of the big kitchen. "A fresh chocolate donut with Claire's special fudge frosting would be a nice accompaniment."

"How about a glass of Sunny Delight in a tall jelly glass and a chocolate pop tart?" Misty smiled. She pushed herself away from the counter and took three glasses out of the cupboard.

"I saw what might be the sheriff's car comin' up the road when I was turnin' down the stairs," said Ben. "You gonna tell 'im what Scooter found out?"

"Yep," said his father. "They need to get the law on this, and we need to find out where John Lawford is." He rose to go to the front door.

The sheriff drank a large mug of coffee laced with sugar and cream while Hank and Angela went over what had happened in the past 12 hours. He listened with his hat in his lap and his glasses pushed over the top of his head. He was tired, and his eyes blinked in an offbeat, distracting rhythm.

"Well, no one who was out on watch last night saw anything suspicious. I got reports from about 10 ranchers who stayed awake, watchin'," said the sheriff. "You hear from anybody?"

"The only call we had was from Kevin Belle," said Hank. "Called Charlie early this morning. He was doin' the patrol around his place. Came up empty. Wanted to know if anyone else had seen anything."

"Imagine he's pretty worried—him runnin' those expensive Limousin bulls. Well, to the best of my knowledge, no one saw beans," said the Sheriff. He rocked back in the flexible chair, then pushed himself forward with his hands on his knees and stood, rocking on the heels of his gray alligator boots. He sighed. "C'mon, let's go see what else we can find."

Hank nodded at Misty and Tony. "As long as you have the horses saddled, you might as well follow along. See if you can tell if any cattle are missing."

He started toward his office. "I'll get the pasture counts."

"Why don't I come along in the pickup—in case you want to stay out there after the sheriff leaves?" Angela called after him.

"Sounds good," said Hank from deep in the hallway.

Soon Ben was alone in the kitchen. He moved carefully off the big rocker to turn on the television that rested on top of a cabinet opposite. As he reached for the power button, the telephone on the wall clanged again, and he limped over to answer it.

"Ho," he said. He strained to hear. There was a jumble of voices, but he couldn't make out any words. He was just about to return the receiver to its hook, thinking it was the rolling background racket of a room of solicitors, then he heard a man's voice shouting, "Hello! Hello!" It was John Lawford.

"Mr. Lawford, is that you?" said Ben.

"Yep, it's me. This Tony or Ben?"

"It's Ben, Mr. Lawford."

"Need to talk to Hank."

"He's not here. He just went out to the pasture…"

"I don't have but a minute. Tell him this. There're some papers in a hidden drawer in my desk. The drawer is under the left-hand slide, and the key is taped on the bottom of the first drawer on the right. Tell Hank to find 'em and bring 'em home. I'll call t'night to tell 'im what to do with 'em."

Ben thought he heard the loud voice of someone on a public address system in the back—saying something in Spanish. "Where are you, Mr. Lawford?"

"Never mind where I am. Just get that message to your dad."

"But Mr. Lawford, I think Scooter has already..." The line clicked, and a dead buzz strung itself out in Ben's ear.

Ben dialed his mother's cell phone.

"Angela West."

"Mr. Lawford just called," Ben said quickly. "He wanted to talk to Dad—wanted him to go over to his house and get some papers out of a hidden drawer in his desk. I started to tell him that Scooter had already found those papers, but he hung up before he heard."

"Where was he?" asked his mother.

"No idea, but he said he'd call back tonight and tell Dad where to send 'em. It sounded to me like he might've been in an airport or somethin'. There was a loudspeaker in the background—and they weren't talkin' English—sounded like Spanish maybe."

"Mexico?" said Angela.

"Could be," said Ben.

"Ben," said his mother, "The number for Scooter's message service is under the phone in the hallway. Leave Scooter a message telling him exactly what Mr. Lawford said."

In less than half an hour, Scooter called back. Ben picked up the telephone in the hallway as he made his way toward his bedroom to dig out some cut-off jeans. He recounted the conversation he had had with Scooter's father.

"Well, thank God he's O.K." Scooter was talking on the outside of the mellow drone of the motor of an airplane. "I'm with my friend, David—this is his plane—we're just waiting to be cleared to take off from Flagstaff. I should be at the ranch a couple of hours after we get in the air."

"You must be sittin' in somethin' that's a lot faster than Hooter," said Ben.

"Ohhh yeah. Henry's new Citation is pretty speedy transportation. Uh-oh, we're cleared. Gotta go."

Ben called his mother to tell her that Scooter would be at the Lawford place in a couple of hours, then he hung up the telephone and started toward the kitchen. All this excitement was making him hungry.

Chapter Nineteen

Ben had just pushed most of the last wedge of pizza into his mouth when the telephone rang again. He chewed and swallowed as much as he could and finally answered on the fourth ring.

"Ho."

"Hello." There was a slight pause. "I was trying to reach Hank or Angela West." A woman's voice.

"You've got the right number, but they're out in the pasture. This is their son Ben. Can I take a message, or do you want my mom's cell phone number?"

"Hi Ben. This is Melissa Sandler. I wondered if you'd heard from John Lawford."

"Well, yeah, as a matter of fact, I just talked to him a little while ago." Ben swallowed the last of the pizza.

"What did he say?"

"Not much," said Ben. "Wanted my folks to get him some papers."

"What kind of papers?"

"Have no idea," Ben was thinking Mrs. Sandler was as nosy as ever. What Mr. Lawford wanted was really none of Mrs. Sandler's business.

"Where was he calling from?" she asked.

"Don't know," Ben answered curtly, then "Uhhh, Mrs. Sandler, your boys aren't on the Lawford place anymore."

Another pause. "Where are they?"

"Well, right now they're under house arrest. I'm not sure where." Ben thought it better that their mother didn't know where the boys were; she might try to break them out again. He told her a shortened version of what happened to them the day before, telling her it was an accident that they fell into the prickly pears. He just didn't want to have to answer any more of her questions. "The sheriff hasn't told anybody where they are—just in case the story they told him is true."

"It's true all right." Melissa Sandler was crying. Ben heard a short tone signaling that someone else was trying to call, but he didn't want to lose Mrs. Sandler, so he ignored it.

"Oh, jeez, Mrs. Sandler, don't cry. The sheriff is takin' care of 'em—makin' sure nothin' happens to 'em." He paused. "Honest, no one knows they were even on Mr. Lawford's place except the sheriff, his deputy, my family and the Coopers, and none of us will say anything t'anyone." His face flushed with guilt as he thought about the men who had herded them through the cactus bed. They knew.

She cried softly for a few seconds, then sniffed. "Ben, John Lawford is in Mexico. The boys' father went down there—ran away. John went down there t'find him. Thought he could get him to come back and talk to the FBI or someone, so we could clear the boys and get our family some protection."

"Sounds like a good plan," said Ben.

"John said he'd call me, but I haven't heard from him. I was getting worried."

"Well, he was O.K. as of a little while ago. Scooter's on his way here. Want him or my folks to call you?"

"No, I don't want anyone to know where we are. I'm calling from a pay phone at a rest stop. We're pretty scared."

"Well, things are pretty tense around here too. I didn't get the whole story out when I was tellin' you about our walk through the prickly pears. What happened to me and Brett and Brady might have somethin' to do with some rustlers who are stealin' yearlings from the ranchers around here."

"Stealing yearlings? Cattle?" There was silence on the line, then she said, "A yearling comes in a pretty big package. How would they do that?"

"We're not sure. Do you know anyone who drives Humvees?"

"I'm not sure I've ever even seen a Humvee."

"Yeah, well, uh, Mrs. Sandler, I hope you don't think I'm bein' nosy, but I need to ask another question. What's the deal with the big Arabian that's runnin' with Mr. Lawford's herd? The boys said he had somethin' to do with how you paid their lawyers."

Silence, then a long sigh. "Ben, tell the boys I love them." She was gone.

Ben tapped the switch hook, then dialed his mother's cell phone. There was no answer, so he dialed the number for the bag phone in the pickup. His father answered, and Ben and told him of his conversation with Melissa Sandler.

"Well, that explains where John is. I'm just afraid he might be mixed up in somethin' that's bigger and meaner than anything he could imagine." Hank thought for a moment. "Ben, we're just about finished here. The sheriff left a few minutes ago. He's on his way over to McAndrews' to check that Dutch Belted for anything he mighta missed before. Jimmy still has him in the cooler." There were a few seconds of static, then his father's voice came back. "Misty and Tony are still down in the south pasture countin' cows. We're on our way down there now. Charlie and Claire should be comin' home from church pretty soon, so I think I'll send the kids home. Your mom and I think we'll go on over to Lawford's and meet Scooter. You doin' O.K.?"

"Yeah, I'm fine."

"O.K. You call if anything changes."

"Yo," said Ben. After he had replaced the lampshade-shaped earpiece back on its hook, he hobbled to the refrigerator, retrieved a gallon container that was about one-third full of milk and gulped it empty. Then he collapsed on the rocker, staring at the old wall phone, wandering what would come next.

Chapter Twenty

It wasn't the telephone that next brought Ben out of his chair. Half an hour later, the sound of tires crunching along the drive made him hobble down the hall to see who was coming. He hoped it was Charlie and Claire. He was anxious to have someone on the place besides his poor sore self. When he looked out, however, he saw Danny McFarland's little gray pickup pulling to the side of the house. Ben opened the door and stood there until Danny loped up the steps.

"Where'd you come from?" grinned Ben.

"Just happened to be in the neighborhood. Tried to call a few minutes ago, but couldn't get through."

"I was on the phone. Come on in." Ben stumbled backward, so Danny could pass.

"What happened to you. You seem like you're limping or something."

Ben pasted his lips together and gave a one-sided grin. "I took a little roll in the prickly pears."

"Did you fall off your horse?"

"Nah, it's a long story. You talked to Misty lately?" Ben tossed his words over his shoulder as he led Danny back to the kitchen.

"No, that's one reason I came out here. She wasn't home when I called yesterday, then when she called me back, she didn't want to talk and acted funny." Danny sat tentatively on one of the kitchen chairs. "I thought maybe she was p.o.'ed at me about something."

"She's not mad," said Ben. "It's just been really crazy around here—you know, worryin' about those Humvees and all. We've started a ranchers' vigilante group to look out for any strange things goin' on."

"Really? So have you found out anything?"

"Nothin' I can talk about."

Danny paused, then asked, "So how'd you get in the prickly pears?"

"Well, I was on the ATV and..."

"You wiped out." Danny finished Ben's sentence.

"Sorta."

"Where were you?"

"Up north."

Danny waited for the details, but Ben said nothing. Instead he picked up the tweezers and magnifying glass that were on the hassock and started picking stickers out of his shins.

Danny had a dissatisfied look on his face; he wasn't used to having to encourage Ben to talk. Finally he said, "So, where is she?"

"She's out in the pasture with Tony. They're checkin' the cattle. Should be home before long."

"Did the new phone work O.K.?"

"Yeah, it's fine, but Dad has it in his truck. Misty and Tony are on horses, and they don't have a cell."

Danny scowled, leaned back in his chair, and stared at Ben.

"You want anything to drink or anything?"

Danny shook his head. "Gees, what's goin' on Ben?"

Ben looked up, set his jaw and gave his best Godfather imitation. "If I told you, I'd have to kill you."

Danny snorted, and then the wall telephone clanged again.

"Can I get that?" asked Danny.

"I'd better, I guess." Ben walked gingerly over to the telephone. "Ho," he said when he had the handset to his ear.

It was Scooter. "Ben?"

"Yup!"

"Your folks there?"

"Nope, they're on the way to your place to meet you," said Ben.

"Well, we're a ways past Stoop's Corner." Ben could hear the drone of the plane and an unusual echo in the broadcast on Scooter's cell phone.

"That was a fast trip," said Ben.

"Yeah, well, as we were descending, getting ready to land at the ranch, we spotted two Humvees and a blue pickup pulling a horse trailer headin' straight north on the county road—toward your place." There was a crackle of interference, then "I don't wanta follow them—don't want them to change their plans. I called the sheriff. He's in the middle of a well-deserved breakfast. He wants to know if you folks can call the ranchers. The sheriff might need some backup to corral these guys. No idea where they're going."

"Sure, I can call 'em. Waddya want 'em to do?"

"Just head for that county road. If they see them, keep them in sight until we find out what they're doing. Might be able to catch them in the act. Tell

195

them not to take any guns and not to confront them. The sheriff and the patrol guys will do that. You got the sheriff's number?"

"Yeah."

"Make sure each one of them has it, so they can call him and stay in contact if they see anything."

"Will do," said Ben. "Uh Scooter." Ben turned his back to Danny. "I know where your dad is. Someone called to tell me. He's in Mexico."

"What's he doing there?" asked Scooter.

Ben looked at Danny. "Uh, my mom'll fill you in when you get to the ranch."

"O.K.," said Scooter.

"Over and out," said Ben.

After he hung up the telephone, Ben started toward the hallway, then glanced back at Danny. "I guess I might need your help," he said. "Come with me into my dad's office. There are two phone lines in there, and we have some phone calls to make."

Danny and Ben were back in the kitchen drinking hot chocolate and dipping crackers into a can of cherry pie filling by the time Misty and Tony pushed open the back door. Misty's face was flushed red from riding, and Tony's hair stood up on his head from the electricity generated when he whisked off the hood of his sweatshirt. They took off their boots and hung their coats on the pegs that lined the back entrance.

Misty skipped over and thumped into the chair beside Danny. "I was pretty surprised to see your pickup," said Misty. "What's up?"

"Nothing. I just felt like driving out here. I tried to call first, but your line was always busy," said Danny.

Misty stretched out her legs and put her stockinged feet on Danny's knees. "Did Ben tell you anything about what's been happenin' around here?"

"I told him about what we think are cattle thieves," said Ben emphatically. "He helped me call all the ranchers, 'cause Scooter spotted two Humvees and a blue pickup with a horse trailer goin' north on the county road. The sheriff wants the ranchers to keep a watch on 'em until he can get here."

"Whoa, that's pretty exciting. Where on the county road?" asked Tony.

"Just south of Stoop's Corner," said Ben.

"Did you reach all of 'em?" Tony put two cups in the microwave—hot chocolate for Misty and for him.

"We talked to everybody but Kevin Belle and Bill Hendren. Left messages for them."

"This is gettin' pretty serious," said Misty. "Tony and I did a count on the two near pastures. We think we're missin' ten of the late yearlings."

"Does Dad know?" asked Ben.

"Not yet," said Misty. I s'pose I'd better call him. He's not gonna be happy."

"I just talked to him," said Ben. "He and Mom decided they wouldn't join the ranchers—that they'd go on over to meet Scooter. I think you can get 'im on the phone in the pickup."

Misty went to the old black kitchen telephone and dialed the number of the bag phone. She stood for a few seconds until a message came over telling her that "the cellular telephone customer you are trying to reach is not available..."

"They must be at Scooter's already," she said as she turned the dial again.

"Hi Scooter," she said after a few seconds. "Could I talk to my dad?"

A pause. "Well, I couldn't reach 'em on the cell. When they get there, would you have my dad call me?"

"Thanks. Bye." She hung up the telephone.

"They must be out of range," she said.

"Never been out of range with the bag phone before," said Ben.

"Well, they might have stopped or something. I'll try again in a few minutes."

"Claire and Charlie home yet?" asked Tony.

"Nope," said Ben. He looked at the clock. "One o'clock. They're usually home by now."

Misty bent forward to drink the hot chocolate that sat steaming on the table in front of her. She took a sip then leaned back again and started chewing on her lip. "You don't suppose those guys are going after the horses, do you?'

Ben shrugged. "Who knows? They're certainly goin' in the right direction."

"You mean the *horse,* don't you?" said Danny.

"Well, sort of," said Misty. "But there are a couple of mares that are by themselves in a small pasture that could also be a big attraction for horse thieves. They've been isolated and I think they'd be pretty valuable if you had their papers."

"Are you sure those horses are still there?" asked Danny.

"The stallion was there this morning when Tony and I went to check."

"But you didn't see the mares?"

"We would've had to go quite a bit further into Lawford's ranch to check on the mares. We decided to come home. I'll ask my folks about 'em when they call."

Twenty minutes later the telephone rang. It was Scooter. "You heard from your folks?"

"No, we haven't," said Misty. "They aren't at your place yet?"

"No, and I tried to reach them in the pickup too. No answer," said Scooter. "You heard from the sheriff?"

"Nope, and Claire and Charlie aren't home from church yet either."

"It's two o'clock. They should be back by now. Did you try their cell?"

"No answer," said Misty. "Couldn't you have your friend fly over to see if he sees anything?"

"He's gone. Has to be at work tomorrow. He was going to stop in Kilpatrick to refuel then start back to the West Coast."

"Oh, I see."

"I'll call the Sheriff and see if he knows anything. You kids sit tight."

"O.K. Bye."

A few minutes later the old black phone clanged again. Tony answered. It was Scooter. "The sheriff says those guys have guns—shot at Bill Hendren's truck and flattened his tires. The last time anybody saw them, the caravan was going hell-bent toward your

199

place. The sheriff hasn't seen anything of your folks, or of the Coopers. The Sheriff, four patrol cars and the 'copter are on their way, but they're still out about 20 minutes." He paused. "What transportation do you have left there?"

"Dad's SUV, the old Range Rover, Danny's pickup, the brown truck…"

"You kids better come over to my place. What's the best way to get here with the least chance of being seen?"

"Well, we should probably go off road and around the back of the hills—like we went this morning on the horses."

"Yeah, that's what I thought too." Scooter lowered his voice for emphasis. "Take the Range Rover, and get started. Now!

Chapter Twenty-one

"Scooter says we need to get out of here—now! I'll explain when we're in the car. We're going off road, so we'd better take the Range Rover."

Tony was rummaging through the drawer where they kept the extra keys. He threw a set to Ben and said, "You okay to drive?"

Ben nodded. "I think I got 'em all out of the bottoms of my feet."

Within two minutes, they were heading out across the pasture in the big faded-gray Range Rover. Ben was driving. Tony was next to him in the front seat, relating everything Scooter had told him. Danny and Misty were in the seat behind.

"If they have a horse trailer, they gotta be after the horses," said Misty. She pushed her body sideways into the back of the seat as Ben ground the heavy vehicle over a bed of rocks and up the side of a hill.

"They could be using the horse trailer to haul cattle," said Danny.

"Yeah, that's what I thought too," said Tony, "but who knows? We know they were chasin' the horses before."

"Well, we might see the horses on the way—unless the herd has moved on," said Misty. As Ben took a narrow shortcut between two big cottonwoods, she closed her eyes. All she could see before her were the two Humvees grinding deliberately into the herd of Mr. Lawford's exquisite Arabians. She would do whatever she could to keep those men from the horses—especially Mirage.

In less than 15 minutes, they were at the fence Misty and Tony had been riding a few hours before. When Tony jumped out to open both sides of the gate, so the Range Rover could make its way through, Misty and Danny got out too.

Misty climbed the split-rail fence to search the hills for the horses. Danny helped Tony with the gate.

"I think I see something over by the windmill. I wish I had the binoculars," Misty shouted.

"I think Mom has some in here somewhere," said Ben. He opened the big glove box in the dash, quickly looked under everything, then reached under his seat. He brought out a small leather box. "Here's a set—the ones Grandpa Lewy used to use," he shouted back. He buzzed the window open and tossed them to Danny who was standing beside the car. Danny took them to Misty who leaned down from the top of the fence.

She took out the small silver binoculars, adjusted them carefully, looked to the south, then yelled, "Can we go over there?"

"That's as good a way as any," said Ben. She jumped down as Danny and Tony closed and latched the gate. When they were all belted into their seats, Ben made a motor noise in his throat, shifted into drive, and with the light touch of a born navigator, gunned the big machine through a roller-coaster ride over the hills.

"We go any further and they'll start runnin'," said Ben as he pulled to a quiet stop about a half-mile from the herd. A few of the horses were standing at the edge. Their ears were up, and their stance alert; they were looking in the direction of the Range Rover, which was now brown with dirt and mud.

"We can't stop here. We need to get to Scooter's." Tony turned in his seat to look at Misty. "They're as inaccessible here as they would be anywhere. Nobody but you would even know they were here."

"I'd feel better if Mirage were somewhere closer to the house where we could watch him," she answered.

"His name's Mohit—and we can't drive the whole herd with this one car," said Ben.

"I could ride him up to the house if we could find him," said Misty. She leaned over the seat to see if there was anything in the back she could fashion into a lead. She pulled up an old sheet her mother had used to wrap a picture frame she had purchased at an estate auction. Quickly, she jammed it over a screwdriver that had been lying at her feet and made a small tear. She then put her finger through the hole and ripped the hem from both ends of the sheet. She tied a knot in the middle and began testing it for strength. It made a wide and sturdy lead of about 11 feet. When she was sure it was solid, she made a leap out of the Range Rover and wrapped the length around her left hand.

"How do you know he can be ridden bareback?" asked Danny as he slid across the seat and followed her out the door.

"I don't. But I'm gonna try." Misty started to walk toward the herd of horses, then suddenly she stopped and turned back. She went to the back of the Range Rover, raised the end-gate, and leaned in.

Danny and Tony came around to watch. She was turning the combination lock on her mother's big safe that was bolted to the bottom of the bed of the trunk. In a minute, the door swung open, and Misty pulled out the old saddle she had found under the quilts two days before. She rolled it under her arm and started back toward the horses. Tony walked tentatively behind her. "Misty, you can't do this." He lengthened his steps, caught up to her and tried to grab her hand. "Besides, that saddle's really valuable."

"I can try. You boys just stay here 'til I get on his back, then you go on to Scooter's." She turned back to glare at him. "I'll be fine, and I won't hurt the saddle."

From the look on her face and the sound of her voice, Tony knew they would have to tie her up to keep her from going after Mohit, and he wasn't quite ready for that kind of fight. Besides, the horse probably wouldn't let her get close enough to give her a shot at getting on his back anyway.

When she was within 100 yards of the horses, she began a strange, slow-motion dance, three slow paces in scissor-steps, stopping for three seconds to judge the posture of the horses, then forward three paces more.

Tony walked back to the car, and the boys stood leaning against the side of the Range Rover, watching her wind forward. When she was about 50 yards from the herd, the big liver-chestnut with the bloody shoulder walked up the outside of the herd to meet her. He stood picture perfect, beside a giant yucca, his small ears up, poised to gather as much information as possible about the intruder. Misty approached him with her right hand stretched out before her. The stallion stood very still, alert, but unafraid. It was almost as if he knew she was coming to protect him.

When she was about 20 feet from the horse, she stood still. The wind, warmer now in midmorning, swirled around her. Slowly she reached into her pocket, then extended her hand, palm side up. She wished she had a treat to offer.

Mohit angled toward her, using a step that was not unlike the one she had used as she approached the herd, his nose was high, his steps small. When he was close enough, he smelled her empty hand and shook his head, puzzled. She turned her palm to extend the back of her hand, eager to have him gather her smell, to breathe in her scent, so he would feel she was a fellow herdmate, not a predator.

"Sorry, handsome, but I came unprepared," she whispered. Carefully, she raised her hand and touched his nose very lightly. "Would you let me pet you?" He took one step back, but watched as she put her hand in her pocket once more. When she drew it out, he came forward.

The horse nuzzled her bare hand again. This time she raised it slowly and began to smooth his forlock with light, but steady, strokes. Then very slowly, still petting his head, she laid the saddle on the ground and unwound a few feet of the strip on her hand with as little movement as possible, gathering the ends, so the horse wouldn't think it was a snake and become skittish.

Slowly, she put the crude lead to his nose, so he could smell it. He backed up half a step; she stretched it out between her hands and put it to his nose again.

He took another step back, but allowed her to follow and put the strip over his neck. She tied it loosely, then stood for a few seconds to allow him to get used to it. When he didn't toss his head or show that he was fighting it, she picked up the saddle and tugged gently on the lead to take him to a small hillock a few yards away. The big horse hesitated, and the other horses behind him moved nervously, but he followed, his head down, his neck relaxed.

She stood on the sandy mound and raised the saddle to the horse's nose. She let him look at it. He seemed surprised but didn't back away. She held it up, so he could smell it, and she rubbed it on his head and his neck before she finally threw it over his sleek back. He didn't move. She leaned down, gathered the soft leather girth and cinched it loosely with a gentle tug. Bravely, she moved to his other side and checked the strap to make sure it was stable, then she stepped to the top of the embankment. Leaning over, she ran her hand across the saddle and over his rump, softly at first, then with more firmness, testing him, preparing him for the pressure he would feel when she grasped his mane and jumped on his back.

Finally, taking a deep breath, she vaulted so fiercely that she almost slid over the other side, but she pushed herself back to an upright position and sat, waiting to see what the big horse would do next. She hoped he couldn't feel or hear her heart pounding. She didn't want him to know she was nervous, but her hands were perspiring, and even though the air was cold and dry, her face was damp. She sat on the horse's strong back, perfectly still, for at least two minutes, then she leaned down and began again the gentle stroking on his neck. There was a slight ripple in the muscle under her, but she could tell the horse was not surprised by her weight, nor was he taken aback by the fact that there was no hard and unforgiving leather between her and his skin. Silently, she thanked whoever had trained him to the light and supple Arabian saddle.

When her racing heart had calmed a bit, and she could feel the horse steady but restless beneath her legs, she gave slight pressure with her ankles. He moved forward, slowly, at a walk. Her scalp tingled, and she looked down at her hands, surprised at how loosely they seemed to lie, entangled in the long, ragged mane. She could barely feel her fingers, because she was straining so to keep the horse's coarse hair tight between them, her improvised lead still wrapped around her hand. After a short walk, Misty could tell the horse was eager to move faster. She was surprised at how revealing it was to sit in this saddle that was not much more than a pad. She could sense the horse's mood by closing her thighs and leaning slightly forward on his back.

She pushed again with her thighs and calf muscles. The horse began a slow walk. She circled him around the hill, learning how they would work together. As they came around for a third time, she tugged his mane gently to the left and led him away from the herd, wondering if the other horses would follow. They watched intently but stood their ground. Relieved, Misty continued across the prairie for about the length of a football field, then tapped the stallion gently with her heels and said, "O.K., I'm ready; let's blow this joint."

Mohit went into a quick trot that strained Misty's legs, since she had no sturdy saddle or stirrups to support her. She melted into the horse's neck and urged him to go faster by kicking him softly with her heels. He stretched seamlessly into a gallop.

Within a few seconds, she was being ferried across the prairie, the great stallion's gait impossibly smooth as his strides lifted effortlessly and his head rose into the air. He was running a race born of his long and demanding heritage. She turned him by leaning in the direction in which she wanted him to go, pulling slightly on his mane and purring approval when he obeyed. He responded immediately to any direction she gave him. When they were approaching Apple Rock, Misty raised her head and sat high in the saddle. She was getting accustomed to the fluid speed of the horse, and her body and his seemed to be one device, gliding through the whispering grass of the prairie. She looked to the side, and she could see the Range Rover traveling parallel to them, about half a mile to the north. They were about five miles from the Lawford house.

Mohit showed no signs of slowing and hadn't even begun a sweat. Misty was giddy with exhilaration. Riding this horse, she thought, was the most glorious experience of her life. Her body had relaxed to his, and she felt a connection to this animal she had never felt for any other being. She thought back to comments by some of the other ranchers about Mr. Lawford's foolishness about the Arabians. She had heard some of them call Arabians spooky, or unmanageable, or hard to train. Misty smiled slightly and remembered that Charlie had once told her that smart horses are more demanding of those who work with them—that if you have an intelligent and sensitive animal, you have to take the time to be sensitive and use some intelligence. Obviously, whoever had trained this horse had been both. She just hoped he respected her as much as she respected him.

The next time she looked toward the Range Rover, she saw it had closed in and was no more than 100 yards away. Tony was leaning out the window motioning to something behind her. She looked back. Something was following. She looked again. It was one of the Humvees. Then she looked to her left and saw that another Hummer was closing in on that side as well. It was about 100 yards away.

Misty leaned into her horse and whispered, "Ya gotta be good now, boy." Then she sat back in her saddle and motioned to Ben to back off, so she could drive the horse in front of him. He slowed the Range Rover, and when he was back far enough, so that Misty was fairly certain the big vehicle would not frighten the horse, she and Mohit crossed in front it.

Ben understood her plan. "You guys get your heads down." Ben stepped up his speed, blocking the Humvees from following the girl and the flying horse as the two made a path that angled in front of and beyond the Range Rover. It took them onto a narrow pass that trailed over a long, low bluff running parallel to Picnic Rock, which was about a mile away. He parked in front of the entrance to the pass. The backside of the bluff was thick with evergreens, and the front was a sandstone wall. Ben doubted that even those old indestructible Hummers could drive through the trees or get up the wall to gain access to the pass.

The Humvees were within 20 feet of the Range Rover now. Ben pulled on the emergency brake and ducked down in the seat, waiting for them to ram him—or worse, to start shooting. He adjusted the side mirror, using a button on the lower dash, so he could see them coming. The drivers were wearing the same camouflage fatigue caps that Misty and Ben had seen two days before, and their faces were partially covered with oversized, shaded driving glasses. It was impossible to tell what they might look like. The big machines weren't interested in Ben, however. When they were just a few feet away, they veered and roared forward along the bottom of the bluff.

"They think they'll catch her at the other side of the bluff." Ben chuckled.

"Well, we know they don't know this country like we do," said Tony, relieved.

"Why, where's she going?" asked Danny.

"Nowhere. That path just circles around and comes out right back here. They won't be able to tell that, though. I think the best thing we could do is follow 'em, try to head 'em off if they come back here." said Ben.

"What if they have guns?" asked Danny.

"If they have guns, I sure as hell don't want 'em shootin' at my sister," said Tony.

"Well, neither do I," said Danny, "But…"

"Besides," said Ben, "I think our wheels are a whole lot faster than theirs. Don't think those Humvees go over 60-70 miles an hour—90 tops, and it takes them a while to gain speed. We can outrun 'em." He lowered the emergency brake and pulled out to follow the big Hummer.

Up on the bluff, Misty slowed Mohit to a walk and guided him off the path. They squeezed through gaps among the scrub pine and evergreens until they circled around into a crevice behind a large swell of sandstone, mother to a small forest of ragged cedar trees growing in the wide cracks at its base. Anyone coming up the pass would be unable to see her. She drew the horse to a stop and listened carefully. The sound of the motors was tapering into the distance. Before long, she couldn't hear them at all.

"Wadda ya think? Should we wait it out here, or should we make a run for the house?" She leaned down to embrace the horse and remembered how defenseless she had felt when she and the horse were running across the prairie, trying to escape from the relentless machines.

And she had another worry. If she went the back way to the Lawford's house, in the other direction, away from where the Humvees had gone, the terrain was very unpredictable. There were rocks, cracks, prairie dog holes, and patches of very soft and treacherous sand. She didn't want to risk injuring the stallion she was riding; galloping would be out of the question. With a sigh, she threw her leg over the horse's rump, sat sideways, and jumped off his back. Thoughtfully, she tied the horse loosely to a small

211

cedar. "We have to wait here for a while, fella," she said softly.

One by one, she lifted all of the horse's feet and examined them. Each hoof was pristine, healthy, undamaged by his time on the prairie or by their long run. She buried her head in his neck with relief, then stood stroking his damp shoulder until she heard the sound of something tracking quickly up the pass. Her skin prickled, and her breath stopped. She waited beside the horse, more frightened than she had ever been in her life. Then she heard a low voice. "Misty? Misty? It's Danny!"

She let out a long breath of relief and leaned against the wall of sandstone. "Stay where you are," she shouted softly. "I'll come out to get you." Still trembling, she made her way through the trees until she reached the pass.

Danny was sitting on a small log, wiping his face with the bottom of his sweatshirt.

"Up here," she said as she stepped out onto the pass above where he sat. He looked up, then rose and puffed his way up the hill. He stood before her, frowning and breathing heavily. She leaned against him with relief.

"I'm so glad to see you. Where are the twins?" she said with a raspy voice.

"They're off after the bad guys." He looped his arms across her back and kissed the top of her head. "Your friend here is a coward. I didn't want to get shot at."

She raised her head to look at him, her face a mask of panic. "Oh, God, Danny, do you think the boys will get hurt?"

"No, I honestly don't. I'd put my money on those two every time. I doubt anybody could out-drive Ben." He shook his head. "I just didn't want to go along."

"I'm glad you didn't." She pulled out of his arms, took his hand, and led him back into the trees toward the horse.

Chapter Twenty-two

"This is like the end of a good chess game," growled Tony. "We have one queen left; they have two rooks, and the battle goes on."

"Bad analogy," said Ben. "There aren't any kings."

"Oh yes there are. I think our sister just rode off on the king for the whites," said Tony, "and I think we're pretty close to findin' out exactly who or what the black king is."

"Well, your rooks are circlin' back, and I think they're gonna come up on each side of us and try to get us stopped," said Ben as he watched the rear view mirror. "What should we do?"

"We circle around and start back the other direction—surprise 'em—do what they least expect," said Tony.

"Boy, I'm glad Mom had this thing full of gas," Ben said as he shifted down and pressed on the accelerator. The turbo-driven Range Rover roared obediently over the rough, tundra-like terrain, and Ben leaned back in his seat, guiding the big machine expertly, swerving around mounds of rocks and dangerous sloughs of sand. At the top of a flat table of sandstone, he made a u-turn that turned the vehicle on two wheels. The Range Rover settled back into a safe relationship with the ground, and Ben yelled, "Duck!" as he started following his tracks back the other direction. The bigger, clumsier and less responsive Humvees were still negotiating a turn as Ben and Tony shot through their own dust and bumped their way to the far side of Picnic Rock.

"Let's go home," said Ben, and he turned toward the east, toward the Lawford house.

"Yeah, it's kind of dumb to stick around here. We could get killed or somethin', but what about Misty and Danny?" asked Tony.

"Misty should be long gone by now—either that or in a good hidin' place; she knows this part of the country like she invented it," said Ben. "Danny's pro'bly with her. Besides, we're not that far from Lawford's. We'll send some others out after 'em."

The Humvees trailed the Range Rover until it reached Picnic Rock, then they stopped, backed around and started back toward the bluff.

Tony turned in his seat to watch them go. "We need to get help, fast!" said Tony, and Ben gunned the big machine across the prairie toward Lawford's house.

A few miles north of Stoop's Corner, off the county road, another chase was winding down. To Deputy Will, who was watching from the helicopter above, waiting for instructions from the sheriff to close in, it seemed to be happening in slow motion. Larry Lopez and Bill Griese were in Griese's truck and had been watching the horse trailer and the military flatbed ever since they caught up with the intruders coming onto the road after leaving the Diamond W. The ranchers stayed behind them at a measured distance, never getting close enough to allow them to fire a gun at them, never letting them get out of their sights. Ted

Nolde had joined them from behind about two miles into the pursuit.

The ranchers were concerned because they could no longer see the Humvees. They had left the flatbed somewhere between the place on the road where Bill Hendren had lost his tires and the ranchers had picked up the chase. Pillows of dust made a smoky train behind the two vehicles. Finally, after going north for about five miles, the pair split up. The pickup and horse trailer turned west. Bill Griese stayed behind the horse trailer; Ted Nolde followed the semi. The sheriff in his Jeep and two state patrol cars arrived just after their quarry had gone in different directions, but Deputy Will had been keeping them informed over the radio as to everyone's whereabouts.

A quick conversation over the radio decided that Sheriff Calahan would go after the semi with the flatbed, and the patrolmen would give chase to the pickup and horse trailer. The ranchers would drop back to follow. Deputy Will circled above and watched as the sheriff caught up with the driver of the flatbed and blocked the road in front. He thought for a moment the driver might take off across the prairie, and he was prepared to go down to help, but the driver stopped and came out of the cab, hands on top of the fatigue hat.

When the sheriff signaled he had his prisoner under control, Deputy Will turned to the east, the blades of his helicopter cutting the way through the prairie gusts. Soon he was flying above the other four vehicles that were racing over the gravel road toward the hills.

"Should I come down and block the road?" he said into his radio microphone.

"Not yet," answered one of the state patrolmen. "The officer in front of me is using his speaker to request that they pull up. We'll see if they comply."

Deputy Will watched as the big blue pickup slowed. Finally, it came to a stop, and the driver inside pushed open the door and jumped to the ground with hands fluttering in the air. Deputy Will sighed, relieved. He was very glad he didn't have to put himself in a place where bullets were flying. He'd seen plenty of gunfire as a ranger in the Gulf War. So far, as deputy in Basket County, he had never fired his gun, and that was just fine with him.

Slowly, Deputy Will turned his 'copter and swung to the left, so he could land about 20 yards to the south of the blue pickup. The blades above him were going around in lazy circles as he jumped down and walked toward the patrol cars and the pickup. He could see the Sheriff's Jeep, followed by Ed Griese's pickup, coming toward them from the west. Soon the sheriff pulled up. He left his passenger handcuffed in the back seat of his white Jeep and walked over to talk with the officer who sitting in the patrol car. Ed Griese parked behind, and the two ranchers sat in Ed's pickup.

Deputy Will turned back to the patrolmen. One of them was walking toward his patrol car, driver's licenses and auto registrations in his hand. He would run them through the police data bases to get what information he could. The other patrolman was standing in front of the former occupant of the pickup. Ted Nolde was leaning against the bed of his truck, watching carefully as the sheriff helped his prisoner out of his Jeep, and they walked over to the other patrol car.

Deputy Will was surprised to see both of the fugitives were women—tall women—both looked to be about his height—almost six feet. The younger woman stood with a slouch, her hands in her pockets. She was dressed in faded jeans, a red sweatshirt and black boots, and she had one long blond braid that snaked down her broad back. She had big blue eyes and a small, flat nose. Deputy Will thought she looked like the woman Misty and Ben had described as driving the stock truck coming out of Juniper Park the day before. The other woman was slender with short gray hair, long legs in tight designer jeans, a fitted denim jacket with rhinestones trailing down the sleeves, pearl-white cowboy boots, and a very frightened expression on her face. She looked like a city grandmother who got caught on her way to a line dance.

No one was saying anything. The lawmen would not ask the women questions until they had any information that could be gained from their documents.

Deputy Will walked over to hear what was going on.

The sheriff was leaning into the open window on the passenger side of the patrol car. "This woman is from Colorado. Ran her license through—clean record except for one controlled substance charge that was later dismissed—says she's a hairdresser and hasn't done nothin' wrong—says she's helping her friend who has a business deal with John Lawford—says

Lawford welshed on the deal and her friend's tryin' ta make it right."

The telephone in the sheriff's Jeep rang. "Can you get that Will?" he nodded backward toward his SUV. Will walked over, leaned in, and picked out the telephone.

"This is Dep'ty Will." In a few seconds, he turned around and yelled to the Sheriff. "It's Scooter Lawford, you wanta talk?"

"Find out what it's all about," The sheriff said under his arm.

"Talk to me," Deputy Will said into the telephone.

He listened for a minute, then hung up and made a quick turn back to the patrol car. "Scooter needs help, says the two West boys just came bustin' in, said the Humvees were chasin' them and their sister, who was ridin' one of old man Lawford's horses. Says she and the horse are someplace between here and Picnic. The boys decoyed the Hummers into chasin' their Range Rover for a while, but the Hummers turned back. The boys think they're after her and the horse."

The sheriff straightened up and turned his steely eyes on Deputy Will, blinking fitfully. Then he pulled up on each side off his belt and shook his head to the side. His sunglasses dropped off the top of his crewcut and back onto his nose, so they covered his eyes. He adjusted them carefully, then looked back at the helicopter.

"I think you'd better go," he said to Deputy Will, then turned back and nodded at the patrolman in the car. "I think we can handle things here." He turned to look at the state trooper who was standing before the

women. "Why don't you and Ed and Larry and Bill go
with the other state guy and see if you can corner those
guys?" He held up his hand for Deputy Will to wait
while he leaned into the car to talk with the patrolman,
then he looked back. "Yep, that's the plan."

The sheriff not-quite-ambled over to talk quietly
with the other trooper. In a minute, he was escorting
the women to the back of the occupied patrol car, and
the other officer had started up his car and turned on
his lights. The ranchers had backed around and were
ready to follow. Will jogged back to the 'copter.
Maybe he had been counting his blessings a bit too
soon.

Chapter Twenty-three

"This'd be kind of romantic if it wasn't so scary," Misty whispered. She was leaning hard against Danny's shoulder and gripping his hand, trembling slightly. They were sitting against a slab of rock watching the big Arabian nibble placidly on tall, sparse grasses that grew through the cracks in the sandstone.

Misty thought about the heavy low roar that had frightened all three of them as the Humvees had ground up the bluff shortly after Misty and Danny had made their way back to Mohit. They had heard them again as the big machines plowed the circular path back down to the grassy pasture below. The horse had stood, legs spread, rigid and alert until the noise had died down; now he seemed relaxed.

Both Danny and Misty were listening intently for any sound that wasn't part of the local oral landscape, worried that one of the drivers might come searching on foot.

Danny put his arm around her and snuggled her head against his neck, beneath his chin. "Do you want me to take the horse and make a run for it?" he said softly.

"I think we're better off here, don't you?"

"I do, so long as they don't find us," Danny chuckled.

"Aren't you scared?"

"Not as scared as I was in the back of that Range Rover when Ben and Tony started out after the Hummers."

"But we're kind of trapped."

"Maybe, but I figure that by now somebody besides us knows what's happening. Scooter was expecting us to be at the ranch by now."

"I just hope Ben and Tony are O.K."

"I'm sure they are. That's one reason I got out. They have pretty good instincts. I figured I might get them into trouble if I started second-guessing them."

"I'm glad you're here."

"Me too," Danny said as he raised her chin and kissed her softly. "Me too," he said again as he put his other arm around her legs and drew her into his lap.

The horse caught the sound first. He raised his head to look into the sky, his great brown eyes open wide, and his ears flat against his head. In a few seconds, Misty and Danny heard it too—the rolling whump, whump, whump of the helicopter propellers coming toward the bluff. Misty stood to soothe the horse. She held the lead firmly and talked softly into his neck as she caressed his back. Danny rose and circled around to climb out of the crevice and wedge his way up one of the taller ponderosas. In a few seconds, he saw the helicopter, circling low over the bluff, then veering off toward Picnic Rock. It was obvious it wasn't flying at random—that the pilot was following something, or taking direction from someone. Danny raised his fists in triumph, then made his way down the tree.

"Definitely Deputy Will to the rescue," Danny said as he slid down the rock toward Misty and Mohit. "I think I'll go out and sneak along the path in the trees—

see what's happening. I'll come back and get you when it's O.K."

"Sounds good," nodded Misty. Danny kissed her quickly and leaped back up the incline and into the trees.

Misty leaned against the horse and nuzzled against the fiery patch on his shoulder. "I don't know which one I like more—you or Danny," she whispered. Mohit turned his head and nickered softly. Misty grinned. She knew that a horse had to have great trust in a human being to offer to communicate like that. That soft, gentle call was usually reserved for mates or other members of the herd. She rubbed his nose and smoothed his forelock. Soon he settled his chin over her shoulder, and she rested her head on his neck.

Danny moved carefully between the pines, taking care to make as little noise as possible, in case one of the drivers of the Humvees had left his machine and was hiding out in the trees. When he reached the path, he stooped and skittered up the other side, along the edge of the bluff. He peered over the rough sandstone. The noise of the helicopter masked the sound of the old army machines, but Deputy Will was close over the top of one of the Humvees that was grinding back toward the west. The other one had veered off to the north.

He watched as the helicopter herded the Hummer through the tall prairie grasses, over rocks, leveling a stand of small cottonwood saplings and managing steady speed through loose sand and silt. He had never seen a ground vehicle move through obstacles like that. He swallowed hard, but sensed that he no longer had to hide. His enemies were on the run. He pulled himself up and sat, cross-legged, watching the cat and mouse game being played out as the two powerful machines circled below him.

In a few minutes he saw a car and two pickups coming up from the west, traveling in what seemed from his perch like slow motion. But he knew they were going at high speed, because clouds of dust billowed skyward when they came up on the dry patches of clay, sand, and silt where no plants bound the earth with their roots. He watched as they drew closer, and he could tell by the row of lights on top of the blue sedan that it was a patrol car. When it was about 100 yards from the helicopter and its prey, the car veered off to follow the Humvee that had started a track to the north. The pickups headed straight for the machine that Deputy Will was tormenting.

Deputy Will came down low to the back of the Humvee, and Danny could hear his loud broadcast from the 'copter. He wasn't sure what he was saying, but the Hummer stopped, and the driver soon opened the door and came out with his hands on his head. The ranchers leaped from their pickups. He could see that Ed Nolde had a deer rifle in his hands and was pointing it straight at the driver. The sheriff wasn't going to like that.

Deputy Will ascended, circled around and started after the other patrol car and the other Humvee. Danny assumed he was communicating with them on the radio. They were miles to the north by now, and as the helicopter trailed after them, Danny soon had difficulty making them out. He decided it was time go back to Misty and Mohit.

He crawled backwards, like a spider, down to the path, then crossed to the trees. He sorted through the branches, hurrying now, anxious to tell Misty that the coast was clear. But when he reached the place above them, past the trees and the waffled ledge that hid them from view, he stopped.

He could see them, and they had not yet heard him. He watched, and his mouth went dry. It was like something from the movies. They were still, and the silver light that spread through the trees was dancing with dust, creating a sparkling mist. The regal Arabian was standing in the embrace of the tall, slender girl whose eyes were closed and her face half-covered by a fall of long, honey-colored hair. He had never seen anything so perfect as this lustrous portrait of horse and girl among the trees.

But Danny was always honest with himself. He wondered if he would be so moved by the enchantment of the scene below him if it were not Misty, but some other girl embracing the silky Arabian.

Chapter Twenty-four

Scooter and Tony grinned at each other in relief when they received the message over the speakerphone in John Lawford's office. The sheriff told them the Humvees had been stopped, and the drivers were sitting in the back of a state patrol car. He said Danny and Misty had come down from the bluff on the horse; all three of them were just fine. Deputy Will was going to fly Danny back to the ranch where he was going to get his truck and head back to Kilpatrick. Larry Lopez was going to pick up Misty after she returned Mohit to the herd, then they were going back to the Diamond W. He or Bob Griese would stay there with her until the rest of the family or the Coopers got home.

Ben came out of the bathroom just as the sheriff was signing off.

"You hear that?" asked Tony.

"Sure did," said Ben. "Now we just have to find the folks and the Coopers."

Scooter swiveled in his chair to look at Ben, then he turned back to punch numbers on the old tan push-button telephone. He dropped the handset back into its cradle when he once again got the message, "The cellular customer you are trying to reach is unavailable…"

"Try the ranch," he said to Tony.

Tony came forward to perch on the corner of the desk. He dialed his home, the Coopers house, Charlie

Cooper's cell phone, and Claire's cell phone. No one responded.

"Did you tell the sheriff we can't get 'em on any of their phones?" asked Ben.

Scooter nodded. "He said to wait a couple of hours before we get all stirred up. He was pretty preoccupied with what he was doing. Said they'd probably turn up—and he's probably right."

"I think we oughta go look for 'em," said Ben.

"Where do we go?" asked Scooter.

"Well we know where they aren't, cause we've just been there," Ben answered. "I guess we go in another direction."

"Out the county road? Or up north?" asked Tony.

"Either one, I guess," said Ben. "You got any other ideas?

"I wish we could take Hooter," mumbled Tony. He looked over at Scooter. "You know how to fly?"

"I used to be pretty good in a Piper Cub, but it's been a long time, and I don't fly a plane I don't know."

"Ben?" Tony looked up at his brother.

Ben tried to surpress a grin. "You know I could fly her, but Dad'd kill me." Ben looked at Scooter. "He said if he ever caught me flyin' that plane alone before I had a license, he'd take away my horse and my car, and I'd have to feed every animal on the place every day until I was out of high school. And he was dead serious." He looked up at Tony. "You been takin' lessons too. Why don't you take her up?"

"I'd ride with you, but I wouldn't wanta fly with me. I'm not ready yet," said Tony.

"Let's try it on the ground first," said Scooter. "Could be they just had trouble with the truck." Scooter stood up. "I'll take the white pickup. How much gas is left in the Range Rover?"

"'bout half a tank, I'd guess, but it wouldn't hurt to fill 'er up." Ben rocked his cap back and forth on his head, then turned the bill to the back and pulled it tight. "You got any two-ways?"

Scooter swiveled back to face the old roll-top desk. He pulled open a big drawer at the bottom right and rummaged through papers and tools until he brought out a pair of small walkie-talkies that were rubber-banded together.

"What's the range?" asked Tony as Scooter wound them apart.

"Seems like I remember they work up to five miles or so," said Scooter. He opened the back of one of the receivers. "We'll have to find some batteries."

"No problem there," said Tony. "When Misty and I were cleanin' your kitchen, we found a whole drawer full of new batteries of all sizes. Your dad sure believes in bein' prepared."

Half an hour later, after hosing gasoline from the big tank that squatted on stilts beside the Lawford's machine shed, their vehicles were making parallel dust trails across the prairie toward the Lawford's north pasture. They looped back and forth for miles. Scooter used his cell phone to keep in contact with the sheriff to make sure no one had heard from the Wests or the Coopers, and they used the little radios to plan the patterns of their search. After two hours, they returned to the ranch, gassed up again, took some snacks from the many boxes in the pantry, and started out in the other direction, toward the county road.

"Maybe I should have taken the plane, after all," said Ben as he leaned back and stretched his arms from the steering wheel. For over an hour and a half, they had been criss-crossing the south pastures that were part of the Diamond W and the Lazy L. The dusk was closing in, and they were almost to Stoop's Corner.

A trilling signal came from the two-way radio Tony held in his hand.

"You got the Range Rover," said Tony as he pressed the button to release the signal.

"The sheriff just called. Didn't wanta talk over the cell phone about the folks he picked up, but he said Deputy Will has taken the chopper over to the east to look for your folks on that side—has Ted Nolde with him as a spotter." Scooter's voice came from behind a light cover of static. "Why don't we meet at Stoop's corner to decide what we'll do next."

"Be there in about five," said Tony. "Over and out."

The Range Rover was there first. Ben pulled in front of the old building, and they sat on the outside of the lip in the cement where the old gas pumps used to be. Ben could see Scooter coming down the road from the opposite direction.

"I gotta take a leak." Tony opened his door, slid out, and jogged around to the back, between the filling station and the old grain storage building. Shortly, Scooter pulled in and parked on the inside, closer to the old gas station, just across from Ben. He rolled down his window.

"What d'ya think?" Scooter had taken off his cap, and his fancy haircut was pasted down on his head.

"They're still not home," said Ben tonelessly.

"Nope," Scooter said flatly.

"None of 'em…"

"Nope." Scooter shook his head.

Tony opened the door on the passenger side of the Range Rover and slid into his seat. He shivered. "It's gettin' cold out there." He reached for a hooded sweatshirt that was wadded in the back seat and pulled it over his sweater. They sat in silence for several seconds.

"Any ideas?" said Scooter.

"I'm thinkin," said Tony.

Finally Tony said to Ben, "When did you and Dad cut that old cottonwood back?"

"What old cottonwood?"

"That big one in back there," he nodded toward the granary.

"Didn't know anything about it," said Ben.

"Well, it hasn't been too long since it's been done. Took out three or four big branches. They're piled in the back."

"See any tracks back there?" asked Scooter after a moment.

"Nope, I thought about that too, I looked, but it didn't look like anything'd been back there for ages."

"Well, let's go look some more," said Scooter.

Ben zipped up his jacket as he hopped out of the Range Rover to join Tony and Scooter. They shuffled through the leaves and debris. The place looked as deserted and forlorn as always.

"Just a minute," Scooter said as he walked up ahead of them and in back of the big old building to their right. About twenty feet out, he stooped and pushed with his foot on one of the branches that lay on the ground. He came back and looked up at the top of the tree, at the raw place where the limb had been amputated.

"Your dad couldn't have done this without help. You're sure your dad or Charlie didn't mention trimmin' this tree?"

"Nope," said Ben. "And Dad wouldn't waste Charlie's time trimmin' trees."

They all stared at the space between the big cottonwood and the building.

"But you couldn't drive anything into that building if you didn't chop off those branches." Tony said what they were all thinking.

They turned as one to look at the rough wood of the building, at the tiny flakes of paint that were left on the aged siding. Then they walked in tandem to stand in front of the wide doors on the north side. The rusty handles were fastened with a dull steel-gray padlock, and it looked like the same one that had hung there for years. If the big doors were freed, and pushed to swing open, the entrance was large enough to allow a dump truck to drive in and spill its tons of corn or wheat into the elevator that rested just beyond. But there were no tracks, just piles of leaves, runaway plastic bags, plastic bottles, and parts of old brown boxes that had blown into a pile against the door.

Scooter shuffled through the trash and rattled the lock. "Looks pretty solid. Any other way you can get in there?"

"There's a door on the other side. There's a little office there. It's always been locked with a dead-bolt though, to keep kids and stuff out," Ben said as he readjusted his cap. "The key's at home."

Scooter and Tony were already walking around to the side of the building. As Ben had remembered, there was a heavy weathered door and two small windows on either side that had been boarded up long ago. As they were walking toward them, Tony stopped and tugged lightly on the back of Scooter's jacket. "Stop a minute. I wanna see something."

He knelt down and raked carefully with his cupped hands at the loose leaves and brush to clear the area around the door. Soon he stood up with heavy a sigh. Underneath, the debris had been ground into a dappled mat. Even in the half-light of the early evening, they could see footprints in the half-dried mud and broken leaves, lots of them.

"Why don't I go home and get the key?" Ben whispered, his eyes wide.

Tony backed toward them. "I don't think our key will work. You can see places in the wood around the lock where it's been chiseled. I'd bet that's not our lock."

"Let's call the sheriff," said Scooter, and he started walking toward the drive. In a few minutes they were crowded into the bench seat of Scooter's white pickup, their faces pale, and conversation scarce. The sheriff had told them he was over an hour away. He and the

State Patrol were still busy trying to sort out what their prisoners were telling them. No, they hadn't said anything about Stoop's Corner, but he would radio Deputy Will who could be there in just a few minutes. The deputy and Ted would come to help them break into the building.

Chapter Twenty-five

In less than 10 minutes, they heard the whap, whap, whap of the helicopter's blades, and its lights made eerie, rectangular arches as they played against the backs of the two cupolas that topped each side of the sagging building behind them. After Deputy Will put down in a field across the road to the west, he and Ted Nolde came loping toward them. Deputy Will had his holster with his gun and some grenades, and his ever-present cell phone hung from his belt. Ted was carrying a rifle and a large wide-beamed lantern.

"Got any more flashlights?" asked Deputy Will after Scooter and Tony had told them what they had discovered. The prairie dark was closing around them, and because of clouds, there wasn't even the beginning of a moon.

"Angela had an emergency lantern in the back of the Range Rover, and I found this long fella under the front seat," said Scooter. He held them up.

"Can you drive around to the east side and park so your headlights shine on the door?" Deputy Will said to Ben.

"Sure," said Ben, relieved that he was going to be serving the cause within the confines of the steel and plate glass of the Range Rover.

"Why don't you two get in the car with Ben?" said Deputy Will. "We'll holler if we need you." He was carrying something that looked like a crowbar. Ted had a big hammer. Ben was sure the tools were part of the emergency equipment Deputy Will carried in the helicopter.

"It's going to take some effort to get in there. These old storage buildings were built in the '40's, and they were built to last," Ted was saying as they walked off.

Deputy Will and Ted stood in the glare of the Range Rover's headlights, examining the lock on the heavy, reinforced door, discussing how to proceed. Soon, they turned their attention to the windows. They took turns gouging at the sides of the plywood that was nailed over the windows, then prying into the cracks they made. In a few minutes, they had splintered through. Underneath was the window. They smashed it with their bar, then began their assault on the inside layer, heavy planks that had been screwed to the walls. It took them over ten minutes to break through to get enough leverage, so they could play against the grain of the wood and crack through. Once they had an opening as big as a baseball, they dropped in one of the grenades.

"Tear gas," said Tony. "I feel sorry for the poor mice that might be in there."

"Or the people," said Scooter.

Deputy Will and Ed walked a few feet to the side and stood leaning against the building, watching carefully, waiting for the air to clear. Nothing happened. There were no noises from inside, and after several minutes, they returned to the front of the window and took turns whacking at the wood, making the opening larger, so they could see inside. They snapped on their flashlights and turned them slowly to examine the room beyond.

"Any electricity in here?" Ted Nolde yelled back.

"Nope, those wires are dead," Tony shouted back. "Dad had it shut off years ago."

"This room's empty at least," they heard Ted say to Deputy Will, then the two raised the necks of their t-shirts over their noses and hefted themselves over the ledge of the hole they had just made. In a few seconds they had unlocked the door from the inside, swung it open, braced it with a tree branch and disappeared into the darkness.

It was just a few hundred heartbeats later that a strong glow of light emerged from inside the building. Ben groaned. All of their stomachs knotted in fear. They were sure the two had been caught, and whoever was there had turned their lights on them. Scooter and Tony slunk down in their seats, and Ben ducked too as he started the engine of the Range Rover. Within a few seconds, however, Deputy Will was at the door, his face grim and his voice husky as he yelled, "Doc, we need your help."

"Did you find our folks?" yelled Ben as he watched Scooter run toward the building. Deputy Will nodded, but when Ben opened his door, Deputy Will held up his hand in an involuntary gesture meant to stop them from coming in.

The twins sat for a few minutes, swallowing hard, then they looked at each other, opened their doors, walked to the old building, hunched through the door that led into the office, and carefully pushed open the door to the huge storage area. They could soon see where the light was coming from. Their parents' red pickup and the Cooper's white van were parked in the nose of the cavernous building in front of various kinds of old machinery their father stored there. The headlights of both vehicles had been turned on and were shining brightly against the gray wood of the building. Scooter was leaning into the open door of their parents' pickup, and Ben could see his father's legs dangling over the seat. He walked forward then, and he could see his mother and Claire Cooper lying side-by-side on coats and blankets that were spread out on the dirty wooden floor in front of the pickup and behind a line of barrels. Both their faces were ashen and colorless, and both were still.

Deputy Will and Ted Nolde came from behind the van carrying Charlie Cooper. They kneeled and lay him gently beside Claire.

Deputy Will looked up at the boys and put his hand on the telephone hanging from his belt. "I called for ambulances. It'll be 'bout 10 minutes for the one from Littleville, another 30 for the one from Kilpatrick, and they're going to send the Flight for Life from Southbluff, 'cause the other ambulance from Kilpatrick is out at an accident on '92."

He grunted as he got to his feet. "I'd take 'em in, but I think it makes more sense for us to stay here and keep 'em breathin'. You boys know CPR?"

They nodded. "We learned it in Phys Ed," said Tony, his voice a whisper.

"They're still breathin', but we gotta watch 'em. Haven't been able to wake 'em up. Looks like somebody gave 'em a big dose a somethin'."

237

They could see Scooter working over their father, then he stood back and nodded at Ed to come help him. "Let's get him out of here." It took all three men to carry Hank West to a place on the floor beside Charlie Cooper.

Within five minutes, they were all taking turns giving CPR to Angela West and Claire Cooper. Within ten, they were working over the two men as well, trying desperately to keep them breathing until the medics arrived.

Chapter Twenty-six

Misty flipped the telephone shut, laid it on the dash of the truck and stared at the road ahead—away from Larry Lopez who was driving.

"Tony says they think Mom and Dad will be O.K. They're breathing on their own now—and the tests didn't show any brain damage." She took a deep breath. "Charlie seems O.K. too, but they're still not sure about Claire." Misty's voice was weak and shaking. "She's breathing O.K., but she's still unconscious, and they don't like something they saw on the CT scan."

She raised her knees and folded her arms to make a nest for her head. Her hair fell over her face, and she cried without any sound, relieved that her parents and the Coopers were going to live. The last few hours had been the darkest in her life as she had worried for the four people who were her parents. The Coopers had been on the ranch ever since Misty was six. Claire was her friend and often became her mother when Angela was off on business, and Charlie had taught her to ride. They had always been there.

Larry patted her back gently. "We'll be at the hospital in just a few minutes," he said.

As they approached the parking lot of the hospital, they saw the Sheriff's Jeep parked at the front entrance, its red, white and blue lights still flashing erratically across the top. Scooter's white pickup was parked at an angle, taking up two spaces in the front row of the parking lot.

A reassuring aide at the information desk in the critical care unit said the Wests and the Coopers would be in their rooms in about half an hour and they could visit them then. She guided them to a waiting lounge where Tony, Ben, Scooter, Deputy Will, and Ted Nolde were sitting in a row like school children. In front of them, in the middle of the room, the Sheriff was standing with his feet wide apart and his shoulders hunched. He was talking quietly, his voice raspy. When Misty and Larry entered, he turned and nodded, but didn't pause in what he was saying.

"And we've got two women and two cowboys. One of the cowboys is the trainer that leased that Arabian to John Lawford. His name is Gary Murray, and from what I gather, he's a friend of Melissa Sandler's ex-husband, Gene Sandler—grew up with him in Valentine." He stopped talking while Tony and Ben rose from their padded bench to give Misty a hug and then make room for her to sit between them. Larry squatted on his haunches.

"This Murray says he came here to check on the horse cause he hadn't heard from John Lawford in a few days. And I'm pretty sure he was plenty worried because it looks like he had no right to rent that horse out in the first place." The sheriff nodded at Misty. "You O.K.?"

"Yes," she said, her voice just above a whisper.

"This is all off the record, can't be repeated." His gray eyes drilled into Misty's, then Larry's. They nodded. "This is just the story the way it looks right now."

240

His eyelids resumed their nervous flutter, and he went on. "When Murray came here, he brought some friends. The younger woman is from Wyoming, used to live just across the state line. She used to break horses for Murray. She tells me she was in the National Guard until they kicked her out a couple of years ago, and she's the one that owns those old Humvees—bought 'em a while back at a government auction at a depot in Colorado—Pueblo, I think."

"Yeah, that's where they sell old National Guard vehicles that are too old to be used for training or military duty," said Larry.

"She said she used them for show at stock car races. Said the winches on those old Hummers could lift up some of stripped down cars and carry 'em all the way around the track. The crowd ate it up."

The sheriff dropped back and closed the sliding door that opened onto the hall, and then he pulled up two chairs from a table in the corner. He shoved one over to Larry Lopez and sat down backwards on the other, leaning over the padded back. His shiny black alligator boots began rocking in slow, irregular cadence on the carpet. "The older woman, the one who's wearin' all the rhinestones is a beauty operator—well, she calls herself a hairdresser—a cousin of the gal who owns the Humvees. She's pretty scared, never been in trouble with the law before and told us most of what I'm tellin' you."

He cleared his throat. "It seems they were all hangin' around at the State Line bar earlier in the week lookin' for somethin' to do to make some money, since Murray couldn't find John Lawford, and thought he might have to skip the country. He didn't know the horse was right there runnin' wild in Lawford's pasture." The sheriff gave a wry smile.

"The beauty operator happened to mention that she had some new kind of powder that when it gets wet, it loses its color and becomes a real strong, flexible glue that she uses for women who are losin' their hair. She sprinkles it on their scalp, drips some water on it and sticks on some hair that matches theirs. Lasts for weeks. Well, it didn't take long for them to think of usin' it to make some extra money by takin' some cattle. They figured they'd just shave some of the calves hair off their stomachs or somewhere, sprinkle this stuff over the brand, add some water, and stick on the hair to cover up the original brand. Then they'd re-brand—freeze brand—usin' a homemade stencil and liquid nitrogen."

"That makes sense," said Scooter quietly, as if to himself, "The intense cold of liquid nitrogen kills all the pigment producing cells in the skin of the animal, so the brand would show up. And they didn't have to have a branding iron or build a fire."

The sheriff looked at Misty and Ben. "I guess the first time they tried the hair stuff was in your horse trailer that day you saw 'em chasin' the horses. Murray and the younger gal were the ones on the Humvees that day. Tied one of Lawford's smaller calves in your trailer. They shaved some hair off, and stuck it on the brand, just to make sure it'd stick. Guess it worked." He looked down at his hat, then looked at Misty. "They discovered the big Arabian when you saw 'em that afternoon. They went out there lookin' for calves and found themselves a horse, and once they knew where the horse was, Murray wanted to make sure Lawford didn't see him and call somebody. They thought your trailer belonged to Lawford, so they cut your car phone and disabled the phone in the house."

"That explains why Dad's phone wasn't working when I tried to call," said Scooter, "but they must have come back and fixed it. It was working fine when I got there."

The sheriff shrugged.

"But why bother with the Humvees?" asked Larry.

"Humvees can lift a lot of weight—up to 12,000 pounds, and they can go anywhere—worked fine to round 'em up. They'd use a capture gun to tranquilize those big calves and then they'd hoist 'em up with belts around their bellies. While the sleepy yearlings were hangin' there, they could work their magic on the old brands and re-brand 'em—then just plop 'em onto the ramp and push 'em into the truck. There was a gate and short side-rails on the ramp to keep 'em from comin out or slidin' back down. They could work pretty fast that way. I guess a couple of the heavier animals woke up before they got 'em into the truck—started fightin' the ramp. That's why you found those steers with the broken necks. The calves broke their legs, so they took 'em away, broke their necks and buried 'em."

The sheriff paused and squinted, blinking just a bit more slowly. "Could be they just pushed the Dutch Belted out the back of the truck after they realized it was risky to take him to market."

"And they thought that pickin' em off a bunch of ranches, just a few at a time—ranchers might not notice, and it would be hard to get the law after them," said Ted Nolde.

"So who was usin' the grain elevator at Stoop's Corner?" asked Ben.

"They parked' the old military flatbed that transports the Humvees in there after you busted their camp at the Juniper Park. Parked the cattle truck in there too. They found a key for the padlock in the desk after they jimmied their way into the office."

"Where's the cattle truck now?" asked Ted Nolde.

A small, crooked, unpleasant, smile crept involuntarily across the sheriff's face. "That leads us to the part that really bothers me. It was the other guy, the one drivin' the other Humvee today that was the real catch—Kevin Belle—your neighbor and Melissa Sandler's brother. We found the cattle truck inside one of his metal buildings."

He paused a moment as his audience mumbled in bewilderment and anger, then he went on. "They were bringin' the cattle there and planned to leave this morning to go north to feed 'em and sell 'em. I figure they woulda made close to $100,000—not bad for a couple days work."

The sheriff reached down to pick up his hat that lay on the floor beside him. He looked at the ranchers, his eyes winking wildly now to some inner rhythm. "Like I said this is completely off the record, but judgin' from what we found at Belle's place, that fancy ranch ain't been paid for by any corporate sugar daddy like we thought. Kevin Belle's been dealin' meth. We think he's the one that got Gene Sandler started makin' the bad stuff—and the women say he's the one that drugged the Wests and the Coopers."

"Why?" asked Tony.

"'Cause they saw that big flatbed comin' out of the grain elevator. The suspects were movin' the Humvees out—getting' ready to shut down their little enterprise. Didn't expect to see anybody that early in the morning—especially the owner of Stoop's Corner."

"Where were Mom and Dad that they could see 'em pull out?" asked Tony.

"The woman said they were sittin' outside the filling station talkin' to the Cooper's who were on their way to church when the Humvees pulled out. That building has no windows, so there's no way they would have seen your folks pull up. When the guys saw your folks and the Coopers, they walked over and pointed guns at 'em to get 'em to drive into the grain elevator. Then they shot 'em up with some of the tranquilizer they'd been usin' on the cattle."

There was a long, flat silence, shock that one of their neighbors could have betrayed them so.

"What about Mohit?" asked Misty. "Why were they chasing him?"

"The Arabian? As I said, the first time you saw 'em was when they found him. They had no idea he was runnin' with the herd until they came up on those horses when they were lookin' for cattle." The sheriff stood up and put his hand on the back of the chair.

"The second time they were comin' after him on their way back to Belle's ranch, so when they left, they could take him back to where he belonged before he got hurt. I guess Murray was pretty mad that Lawford was lettin' him run wild. And I think Murray was gettin' worried that somebody in New Mexico might get wise to the fact that they had a fake." The sheriff swung the chair back to its place under the table.

"Was Kevin Belle part of that too?" asked Misty.

"I don't think so, but that's what got Gary Murray to Nebraska, and he looked up Belle, because Belle was his friend Sandler's brother-in-law. Turned out they were just two peas in a pod."

"Does this mean the Sandler brothers won't have to go back to the boot camp?" asked Ben.

"I think it probably does. There'll be some legal things to go through before we can let 'em go, but it looks like they were just tryin' to stay alive." The sheriff plopped his big hat back on his head and backed toward the door.

"I guess you know about as much as I do now, but don't repeat any of it. I hope those folks in there are gonna be all right." He nodded at Deputy Will. "We'd better get back to business." He turned and walked out of the room and down the hall.

Deputy Will rose slowly and smoothed down his jeans.

"Thanks Will," said Misty, "and tell the sheriff thanks too."

"Thanks to all of us." he shook his head. "It's been a long day." He took a deep breath and followed the sheriff out the door.

Chapter Twenty-seven

Angela looked up as she put the handset of her slick black telephone back in its cradle. Hank was leaning against the door.

"Well, the girls in Denver think I have a pretty damned effective guardian angel," she looked up at her husband with a glaze of tears in her eyes.

"I'd say you and I had a whole flock of 'em," drawled Hank.

It was Tuesday, only two days after the almost fatal overdose. Angela and Hank had come home the night before, and now they were preparing to coil their work lives around a new and challenging personal obligation. Charlie had been dismissed from the hospital, but Claire had not.

The doctors at the medical center had confirmed that the Wests and Coopers had indeed been poisoned with the tranquilizer the rustlers had used to immobilize the cattle while they belted and branded them. If no damage had been done before the lethal chemical left the victim's systems, they were out of danger, but Claire's brain had been without oxygen long enough that there had been some injury. She didn't seem to remember things that had happened recently, her speech was slurred, and her eyes couldn't focus properly. The doctors were giving her medications to help regenerate the activity of the neurons on her brain, but they all agreed that it would be months, maybe years, maybe never, before she would function at a normal level again.

Angela rose to lay her body upright against her husband. He leaned his chin on the top of her head and said, "What d'ya think? Should the kids go to school?"

"I thought we'd decided last night that they should. It's a late day, so they don't have to be there until 10:00." She rubbed her forehead against his chest.

"I just hate to see them leave just now. I guess I'm still kind of shaky about everything."

She drew back and looked at him with a twinkle in her eye and a tight smirk on her face. "It's usually me who's cautious and overprotective."

"I know," he said without explanation, then in a moment, "I just got off the phone with Scooter. Let's go talk to the troops."

In the kitchen, Misty, Tony, and Ben were standing at the long counter, drinking or eating their breakfasts.

Misty turned as her parents came in. "We're all going in one car today. We won't go back to volleyball or football until things have settled down around here." She wiped her hands on her jeans. "Guess we're going to have to pick up some of what Charlie does."

Hank settled into one of the sturdy kitchen chairs and nodded slowly in a way that moved all of his upper body up and down. "I guess you're right, but if he has to be away long, I'll bring somebody else in."

"Would it be O.K. if we stopped by to visit the Sandler brothers on our way home?" asked Ben.

"Do you think they're still in jail?" Angela poured coffee into a big brown mug.

"Deputy Will thinks they'll be in there 'til the District Court meets—sometime this week," said Ben. "They'll probably charge their dad on the same day."

John Lawford had put Gene Sandler on an airplane in Dallas, and the state patrol had picked him up in Denver the day before. He had agreed to give the drug enforcement officers information in exchange for protection and a lighter sentence.

"Have they found Melissa Sandler yet?" asked Tony.

"Guess not," said Ben, "But when they do, Will says she'll be charged with helping her boys escape from the boot camp."

"Seemed like self defense to me," said Tony.

"Maybe the court will see it that way too," said Angela.

Misty looked at her father. "So I heard you talkin' to Scooter. Will Mr. Lawford will be home pretty soon?"

Hank nodded. "Sometime this afternoon."

"When do you think they'll come to pick up Mohit?" she asked.

"As soon as they can get here, I'd guess," said Hank.

"Can you believe he paid half a million to lease that horse?" Tony shook his head.

"I wonder how he got him, since Murray was playin' under the table," said Ben.

"Scooter said his dad told him Murray passed the horse to him in a parking lot outside a casino in New Mexico. The security men who were traveling with him were inside eating and gambling."

"Where was the fake Mohit?"

"The look-alike was in another trailer in the back. The woman with the long pigtail had brought him up from a horse farm in Tucson. I guess the hairdresser did the color job on his withers."

"What I want to know is where did John get $500,000 cash, and how did he know the horse was the real thing?" asked Angela.

"Fact is, he borrowed the money from a bank in Southbluff," said Hank. "Mortgaged his ranch. He arranged an electronic transfer to pay Murray—to a dummy account Murray had set up with the same name as the legitimate horse farm. But John didn't transfer the money until he'd seen the horse—'til he was sure he was the real thing—and once he had the horse, he hightailed it outa there a back way through the Navajo Indian reservation, so they couldn't trail him and take the horse back. He knew they wouldn't come after him til they had checked to see the money had cleared into their account."

"How's he going to pay all that money back to the bank?" asked Angela, "—and isn't he going to get into trouble? Wasn't what he did illegal?"

"Well, John says he was actin' in good faith, says Murray had all the right papers and everything, and I don't know how the court could prove otherwise, but I'd bet that John knew exactly what was goin' on from the time Melissa Sandler first approached him about it." He shook his head and turned sad eyes to his wife. "He just wanted that horse so damned bad—wanted it for so many years."

250

"What if he doesn't get his money back?" asked Misty. "Will he lose his ranch?"

"Well, John's no dummy." Hank chuckled. "Remember those papers he wanted out of the hidden drawer in the desk?"

"Yes," nodded Angela.

"It wasn't the papers on Mohit that he was lookin' for at all. Had those in the saddlebag with him. He wanted the papers on the broodmares the Sandler boys were joy ridin' on. Both of the mares are due to foal in early spring, and they have a very illustrious father."

"Mohit," said Misty, wide-eyed.

"Nope," said Hank. "The gray—Shadow. Remember he has quite a heritage; son of Ksiezna with the bloody shoulder. John bought those mares and kept 'em in that small pasture with the good fence. The only visitor they had was the gray. He's got a buyer in Texas who wants the chance of havin' a champion Arabian foal and is willing to pay him $200,000 for each pregnant mare—but he wants delivery by the end of the month. That's why John was in such a toot to get those papers—so he could fax them to his buyer to start the authentication process."

"But I thought Mr. Lawford didn't sell his horses," said Misty.

"I guess he does when the end justifies the means," said her father.

Chapter Twenty-eight

When Misty drove home from school on Thursday, she was alone. The boys had opted to return to football practice, since her father had hired Brady Sandler to help out while Charlie was in Southbluff with Claire. The charges against Brett and Brady had been reduced after Mr. Sandler testified, and the boys had been released from jail.

It was a somewhat unorthodox trial. Melissa Sandler had arrived the night before court convened on Wednesday; she was arrested, and the boys and their mother were charged with aiding and abetting the escape of prisoners. The charge was reduced to a misdemeanor, however, and they were no longer to be jailed. Instead, they were ordered to complete six months of social service and stay in the state until the court gave them permission to leave. The judge also ruled that all the trash in the Sandler's yard was a hazard to the public health. He directed them to have it cleaned up by the end of the month. Some of the residents of Littleville had volunteered machines and manpower to help. The judge's ruling ended with a statement that implied the court had been lenient because it looked forward to the resumption of the publication of the Littleville Gazette.

As Misty drove into the yard, her father came out onto the front porch. She pulled up close and rolled down her window.

"Your mom's over at Lawford's," he said. "They've come to take Mohit back. Thought you might want to go over to say good-bye."

Misty nodded her head to one side. "Don't you want to go?"

"I've got some paperwork that has to be done. I'll come later with the boys."

"I'll just go up and change, then I'll drive on over."

He gave her a little salute with his left hand and turned to go back into the house.

The drive to the Lawford ranch was lonely. She wished Danny was with her—or Ben—or Tony. The air was heavy with the kind of smoky dreaminess that often precludes a late-autumn sunset, and for some reason she couldn't stop watching the fences—as though she had never traveled here before. Along the county road, tumbleweeds had been gathered in by endless layers of barbed wire attached to communities of fence posts. For one stretch, a row of crooked branches that had been torn from fallen trees held the wire in their fingers. There were rows of steel shafts painted green—followed by cut-to-order poles that marched on for miles like bald little men. There were intervals of flat planks whittled to points, then a parade of big warped sticks that were old and gray—and square posts—thick and sturdy—waiting for a gate. The split rail fences at the top of the barrow pits at Nolde's pasture leaned defiantly toward the road, the severed spines of friendly Juniper trees, their parts the diameter of her arm.

They all seemed ugly and restrictive, inventions of a devious mind.

When she finally found her freedom along the fenceless gravel that wound toward the Lawford house, she drove slowly, deliberately, until she could see the yard. There were several vehicles parked at angles at the side of the house. Her mother's gray Range Rover was there, so were Mr. Lawford's pickup and Scooter's rented Mafiamobile. There were also two she'd never seen before, a very large, black SUV with oversize tires and gold trim and a dually pickup with a fancy air-conditioned horse trailer behind it. "Fit for a prince," she thought.

She parked the Bronco on the gravel by the barn. She could see Mohit was in the corral. When she walked over to the fence, he nickered and trotted to meet her. Then something moved beside her, and she became aware of a short, dark man sitting on a hay bale just to her right. The horse came closer, and the man stood.

"You must be the girl, Misty."

"I am," she said. She held out her hand and walked toward him. He seemed a little surprised, but smiled widely, showing rows of little teeth, and took her hand when she reached him. His grasp was firm, his fingers like rough cushions.

"I am happy to meet you. I am Girard Paussant, Mohit's new trainer." He had a soft French accent.

"You mean his new Nanny," Misty made a face at the sarcasm in her voice and shook her head. "I'm sorry. That wasn't a very nice thing to say."

"No, it wasn't, but I guess that in a way, that's what I am."

She turned to stroke the nose of the friendly Arabian who was arching his neck over the railing, shaking his head, willing her to come into the corral to be closer. "I'm just not in a very good mood. I love this horse, and I guess if I'm honest with myself, I envy you."

"I understand. I've felt like that for one or two horses myself." He looked at her with truthful blue eyes. "I think I shall very likely feel that way about this horse before long."

It was getting dark. The yard lights came on. She could hear voices coming from people walking towards the barn.

"Girard, what if I cry?" she had her head against the nose of the horse.

"So what's wrong with crying?" he asked.

In a few seconds, people were all around her. Her mother was standing beside Girard Paussant. John Lawford leaned on the fence to her left. Scooter and another man were standing at her back.

"Misty, this is Émil Básel," said Scooter.

Misty turned to look at the man behind her. He smiled at her with soft brown eyes. He was very handsome with a high forehead and light brown hair that was slicked back in an expensive looking way. He wore a mushroom-colored suede jacket and pressed blue jeans.

"Hallo," he said, and offered her his hand.

She took it. It was smooth and warm.

She looked into his eyes. "We've had a really bad week," she said. "And now you're going to take my friend away where I'll never see him." Tears ran down her cheeks. "I wish I could say I'm happy to meet you."

"Misty…," her mother began.

"You know I feel just the same way." John Lawford pushed himself away from the fence to come close to Misty and put his arm around her. She leaned her head against his bony shoulder.

Scooter cleared his throat.

"Would you like to ride him?" said Émil Básel.

Misty nodded her head.

"I'll get the saddle," said John. He started toward the house.

"What are you doing?" asked Scooter. "There are saddles out here."

"Not the saddle he was bred to," said his father as he gimped his way to the house.

"Just a minute," said Angela, "I think the saddle you're looking for is in my Range Rover." She jogged to catch up with him, stood for a minute explaining, hands waving in the air, then she led him over to the back of her vehicle.

Soon, they came up. John was carrying the old, flimsy Arabian saddle. He balanced it on the top rail of the corral and went into the barn to get a bridle.

Misty climbed over, retrieved the saddle and step-by-step settled it on the back of the splendid and powerful animal. She shook her head when John Lawford came out of the barn with the halter.

They started a trot around the corral. It was just as before. Misty leaned down to caress the horse's neck, her fingers firmly entwined in his mane. As they made the third turn, she saw that John Lawford had snaked around to open the gate. Misty smiled at him, then guided the horse through the opening and down the gravel drive. They ran hard until they left the jurisdiction of the yard lights, and Misty was concerned about the horse stumbling into holes or sand. She guided him into a hairpin turn and they trotted back down the drive. She stopped him and sat, looking at her mother, her neighbors, and the legal owner of the horse.

"He's the most wonderful animal I have ever known," she said.

"I feel the same way," said Émil Básel.

"Have you ever ridden him?" asked Misty.

"Oh, yes," said the Frenchman, "but not on a saddle like that."

He turned to John Lawford. "Would you sell it?"

"It's worth over $100,000," said Misty's mother.

"I'll buy it," said Émil.

"It's not for sale," said John.

"You're crazy," Scooter said gently.

"I know," said his father, and he looked up at Misty with a crooked smile that made grooves down one side of his suntanned face.

About the Author

Ruth Foreman grew up on the Wyoming border with the Nebraska Sandhills at her back door, but she has spent much of her life in cities. She has published numerous training manuals and has written documentation and publications for Fortune 500 companies all across North America. Now she has returned to the plains, living in small town along the North Platte River—writing fiction that incorporates her love for the horse country of Nebraska with the adventure that shapes the young people who live there.

Printed in the United States
1438900002B/113

9 781410 768544